I0738797

Praise for Anne Louise Bannon and *Fascinating Rhythm*

Fascinating Rhythm is reminiscent of Agatha Christie or Dorothy Sayers' novels of the time period. A very nice story to cozy up to a fire with and imbibe. Legally, of course.

Literary R&R

Those who love a great (who-done-it) mystery will enjoy Fascinating Rhythm.

Sheri Wilkinson

JuniperGrove.net

Praise for *Tyger, Tyger*

I like Bannon's main character, Brenda, enough to follow her anywhere. Her boyfriend (no! wait! they're "just friends") trains animals for the movies, and between Brenda, the BF and his tiger, "Sweetness," they are a fun, crime-solving trio. I enjoyed this book.

Petrea Burchard

Author of Camelot and Vine

Deceptive Appearnces

Anne Louise Bannon

Healcroft House, Publishers

Healcroft House, Publishers, a subsidiary of Robin Goodfellow Enterprises, Altadena, California, United States of America

Copyright 2017 Anne Louise Bannon

ISBN 978-0-9980838-5-8

Library of Congress Control Number: 2017910897

Dedication

For my parents, Dave and Connie Bannon

September 15, 1983

We hit the rain in Lone Pine, as we skirted up the backside of the Sierra Nevadas on our way to Lake Tahoe. It didn't slow Sid down much, at first, except that U.S. 395 stopped being a freeway for a good chunk after that and being in the mountains and all, even Sid slowed down.

"I hope the passes aren't frozen," Sid grumbled as he finally switched on the windshield wipers.

"It's way too early for snow," I replied, trying to sound more reassuring than I felt.

Neither of us was in the best of moods, although for once, it wasn't because we had been fighting. It was the job we were on. We don't usually get a pick-up assigned to us over a week before we have to make it, and since they asked for both of us specifically, well, that meant the job was going to be more than a pick-up.

The worst of it was that we were doing the job as ourselves and not as our alter-egos, something we'd been requested to do, probably because somebody upline had seriously screwed up. You see, I grew up in South Lake Tahoe and the pick up was scheduled for the casinos in Stateline, literally just on the other side of the border in Nevada. Harrah's parking lot is in California, to give you an idea of how close it all is.

I went back to the magazine I'd been reading from. "You want me to finish this? I mean there are only a couple sentences left."

"I'm listening."

"Okay. Where was I? Oh. 'The ultimate problem with Moriarty's is not unlike the problem with Shanda. The club has all the appearances of a truly great night spot, but it will get you in the end. Parenthesis — I told you to watch out for us nice girls. We only look harmless, ljw, close parenthesis."

"Hattie left that in?" Sid asked. Hattie is the editor of Sid's singles column.

"I told you she was going to. She's been leaving in all my parentheses and wants more." I'd been adding them almost since Sid had started his column, but originally as a joke for Sid only. Then a few months before, this one had slipped through to Hattie and she'd thought it was hysterical.

"Oh. That's right."

I looked at him. "You okay with that?"

"I told you I was."

I didn't completely believe him but saw no reason to say so. Instead, I watched out the window for several minutes, listening to the beat of the windshield wipers. Slowly, a familiar melody slipped through my mind and I began humming.

"Windshield wipers keeping time," I sang softly, then sang it again, trying to remember the rest.

"It starts with 'Busted flat in Baton Rouge,'" Sid finally said. My humming tends to get on his nerves, especially when I can't remember the whole song.

"Oh, right!" I went ahead and sang it from the beginning, with Sid feeding me the lines as needed. He doesn't sing, well, not much.

"When did your folks say they'd be back?" Sid asked as I went into the la-dah-dahs, probably to shut me up. [Oh, yes. – SEH]

My parents still lived during the summers up at the resort they owned off of U.S. 50 and weren't scheduled to head down to their place in Florida for another month yet. Fortunately, they were spending the week in New York visiting my great aunt.

Mama and Daddy think that Sid is merely an eccentric, but wealthy, freelance writer and that I'm merely his secretary. We are, but we're also operatives for Operation Quickline, an ultra-top secret government organization, so secret, in fact, that even my family doesn't know that it exists, let alone that Sid and I work for it.

"That's just it, they didn't say," I said. "Mama said something about playing tourist in Boston while they were on the East Coast, but I don't think Daddy's going to go for it. They should be gone through the weekend, though."

Sid swore under his breath as he eased onto the brakes again.

"I'm sorry, but I can't tell my parents what to do," I said, feeling a little defensive.

"It's not your folks," Sid said, braking again. "We're just making lousy time."

We had left later than we'd intended after a small dust-up over whether I was spending ten hours in a car fully dressed in business wear. Sid had agreed to let me go casual since I had conceded to driving up when we could have flown. Sid had said that since we were going as ourselves and odds were decent we'd need a car once there, we could at least take his 450 SL.

Sid does have a lead foot [So do you – SEH], and in spite of the rain, we actually made it to Stateline in just over eight hours, my best time ever. I have to admit, I was a little excited about staying in the casino where we were going to make our drop. I'd been to the casinos often enough, but who stays in the hotels in their hometown?

We had a two-bedroom suite, too. That had been the hotel's idea. We were also there to interview the hotel manager for an article for a major airline's in-flight magazine, and the manager insisted on setting us up in their best room instead of the two I'd requested. It wasn't exactly discreet, but Sid and I figured that with me being a former local, discreet was not on the agenda, anyway.

We parked in the hotel's main lot and carried our luggage in on our own. Sid checked in, got our keys, then held me back before I followed the bellman to the suite.

"I'm going to call in and set things up," he said,

taking off his tan overcoat and handing it to me. "Why don't you get changed and wired up and meet me down here?"

"Dinner?" I asked hopefully. It was past six-thirty at that point and I was starving.

Sid's eyes rolled. "You've been nibbling all day, not to mention how much you ate at lunch."

I blinked twice.

"Oh, alright." Sid pulled out his thin black leather billfold. "For the tip."

He handed me a couple fives. He'd chosen to wear his usual three-piece suit, shirt, and tie. The way he held his suit jacket closed told me he'd already put his shoulder holster on, though when he had, I wasn't sure. Driving in one isn't exactly comfortable and we'd made our last pit stop in Bishop. I couldn't see if he'd gotten his earpiece and transmitter on, but then, you can't really see the earpiece unless you look really carefully for it.

"Go ahead and change, too," he said. "It'll give us more options for the pickup."

"Okay."

With a nod, Sid moved off into the casino, while I followed the bellman up to our suite.

It was huge, decked out in Southwestern pastels, with a sunken floor in the center of the main room, containing a huge circular sofa. The bedrooms were on either side of the main room. I put Sid's trench coat on the rack next to the door as the bellman, who looked like he was barely out of high school, brought our two suitcases and carry-ons into the one bedroom.

"Uh, excuse me," I called out, anxiously. "Two of those are mine and they belong in the other bedroom."

"Oh. Sorry. Uh, which bags?"

"Happens all the time," I sighed.

I do get very tired of people assuming Sid and I are lovers. We may live in the same house – long story how that happened – but we are strictly housemates.

I let the bellman wait while I decided which room

I'd take. They were both pretty luxurious, with huge bathrooms each containing a sauna. But I let Sid have the one with the rock spa tub. I figured he might want to bring some company back to the suite somewhere along the line and was feeling generous.

I gave the bellman the tip, then went back to my room to change into a dark-blue paisley skirt and light blue velveteen Edwardian-style jacket with puffed sleeves and short peplum. I'd trimmed it with dark blue braid and it certainly stood out. I wear my hair fairly long and permed, and picked out the curls, then slid a small piece of spring steel behind my ear.

Unfortunately, the jacket was too fitted for me to carry a shoulder holster, but I had my S & W model thirteen revolver in my monster of a purse. The thing was huge, but it carried everything I needed and then some. I strapped a twenty-two automatic to my thigh, high up under my very full skirt. My transmitter, I clipped to the inside of my skirt, adjusted the microphone inside the jacket's collar and slid the earpiece into my ear. I took one last look in the mirror, then turned the transmitter on.

Immediately, the noise of the casino filled my ear.

"I'm wired and ready," I said, picking up my purse.

"Come on. Bust for me," Sid grumbled, letting me know where he was without letting anyone else know he was wired.

Good thing, too, because the pit bosses are really looking for that sort of thing – you'd be surprised what people do to cheat.

Once I got downstairs it was easy to spot Sid. Okay, the man is particularly handsome, with dark wavy hair, bright blue eyes and a cleft in his chin. He's not big, just three inches taller than me and I'm average. It also helped that he was playing at a twenty-five dollar minimum bet table. Those tables are almost never crowded, except on at peak weekend or holiday hours. In fact, there was only one other player there.

Sid looked up and smiled as I approached.

"Doing okay?" I asked.

"About even," he replied. He signaled a hit to the dealer and winced as he busted. "Oh well. Time to move on."

He gathered up his chips and a drink glass filled with something clear and ice.

"What do you want to do?" he asked, slipping gracefully off the stool.

"Dinner. I'm starving."

"You're always starving."

Which is true. I am. I'm one of those lucky types that can eat like a horse and never get fat, a fact which mystifies Sid, who can't.

"So when's the pickup?" I asked softly as we made our way out of the casino.

"Between nine-fifteen and nine-thirty. You're making it. Just put your purse on the bar in the Keno lounge."

"Oh, good, we've got time for the buffet."

Sid all but gagged. "On your own time, please. They have a nice seafood restaurant here."

"Okay, that sounds good."

Sid shook his head. But I will give him credit. He almost ate like a normal person. Sid is a complete health nut. No red meat, no refined sugar or starches, no fat, small portions all the time. Not that I don't like healthy food. I do. I just like all the other stuff, too. He had grilled salmon, steamed vegetables, no potato, and salad with oil and vinegar on the side. I indulged in surf and turf, creamy dressing on my salad, and loaded up my baked potato with butter and sour cream, and dunked every bite of lobster into luscious drawn butter. Sid sighed but didn't say anything.

We finished around eight-thirty and lacking anything better to do, went over to the Keno lounge. The casino was crowded with conventioneers – a trade association for manufacturers of recreation products was having its annual meeting at the casino that weekend. Sid and I were hard-pressed to find a place to sit but did manage to find a booth away from the betting window and across from the bar.

"I don't think I'm ever going to figure this game out," I grumbled, trying to read a brochure about Keno in the dimmed light.

"Hm." Sid was checking out a woman in her mid-forties sitting a few tables away and trying to look as though he wasn't checking her out – not Sid's usual *modus operandi*.

Which was odd, because she was definitely checking Sid out and with considerably more interest than the other women in the bar, who believe me, were checking.

"What's going on?" I asked.

"Irony of ironies," Sid said with a weak smile. "You know how worried you've been about running into someone you know?"

"Yeah, but I've never seen her before, assuming you mean that woman over there."

"That's because she's someone I know. Or knew."

Sid cussed softly as she got up and made her way over. There was something almost stunning about her, although she didn't have that glamorous look. Her hair was cut short into a wedge and she was wearing a nice, but predictable, dark business suit. It must have been the way she carried herself.

"Oh, my lord, Sid Hackbirn!" she said, smiling happily as she got to the table.

"Della, well, I'll be damned." Sid scrambled to his feet. "What are you doing here?"

"I'm here for the meeting." She held up the badge she was wearing. "I'm VP Finance for Sunland Products. You?"

"I'm here doing a story," Sid said. He waved at the booth. "Please, join us."

"Thank you."

Sid glanced at me and I moved over on the bench as Della slid into the booth ahead of Sid.

"This is my secretary, Lisa Wycherly," Sid said.

"Lisa, this is Della Riordan."

I was waiting for her to question Sid having a secretary – everyone tends to assume he's made his money by writing, which is ridiculous because writing does not pay very well at all. But she didn't.

"Wycherly?" she asked, looking at me carefully. "As in the sporting goods store across the state line?"

"Yeah, that's my dad's store," I said, hesitantly. "He and my mom own the resort out here, too."

"Your father is a good client," Della said.

"Sunland Products. You guys make trail food," I said, even though I was still puzzled. I knew the product line from running my dad's store summers while I was in college. But the big chains carried Sunland, too, and Daddy didn't carry all that much trail food.

"My goodness, Sid, you've done well for yourself," Della said, ignoring me. "What happened to your glasses?"

That placed Della way back to Sid's early college days, at least. He'd gotten his money around then. Sid is extremely near-sighted and hates wearing glasses, so the contact lenses were one of his first indulgences.

"I inherited some money," Sid said, "and promptly got contacts. You seem to be doing rather well, too."

"Well enough," Della sighed. "I still miss teaching, but I can't complain about the compensation for executives."

"Yeah, I'd heard what had happened. So, are you married? Single?"

Della chuckled. "Still single. You?"

Sid laughed lecherously. "Very single and always open."

"Still audacious, too, I see." She glanced at me. "How long have you two been together?"

"I've been working for Sid for a year," I said, my tone getting frostier than I'd intended.

There was something about the way Sid was looking at her. I had a feeling this wasn't just any old past fling.

"Lisa is strictly my secretary," Sid said with a teasing edge to it. "Not for lack of trying on my part."

"You can say that again," I grumbled.

"What?" asked Della.

Sid sighed loudly. "The woman has morals. Can you believe it? In this day and age?"

I put my hands up. "Okay. Got the hint. I'm leaving. Della, nice meeting you."

I grabbed my purse from where it had been sitting under the table next to Della's feet and scooted out of the booth and off toward the bar. I checked my watch and sure enough, it was coming on to nine-fifteen. I knew Sid was giving me an excuse to leave, but I was annoyed at how he chose to do it.

"Snippy little thing," said Della's voice in my ear.

"I wasn't entirely fair," said Sid. "I was baiting her."

I did my best not to glare in his direction and plopped the monster purse on the bar next to me.

"And she does come in for a lot of grief because people keep assuming we're sleeping together," Sid continued.

"I don't know whether to be impressed or horrified," Della said.

"Be impressed. It's not easy for her. Or me."

"I'm surprised you've kept her around. That's not like you, Sid. Or it wasn't."

Sid laughed. "It's still not like me, and if you give me half a chance, I'll prove it. But Lisa's different. I don't get it, but it seems to work out well for us and I'm content."

"Well, bully for you, dear." Della's voice turned deeply sour. "People with morals are why I'm not teaching anymore."

"Lisa's not like that. She doesn't judge, and lord knows, I've given her more than enough reason to." Sid gently took her hand as I tried not to squirm. I knew it was about to get intimate and while we needed to stay wired, I wasn't wild about listening in on his latest conquest.

Except this was different.

"I wish I could have been there when Crowley blew the whistle on you," he continued.

"He was lying, you know," Della sighed.

"That doesn't surprise me." Sid paused. "I, uh, hope it didn't get out about us. I'd hate to think that what we had got you into trouble."

"What we had was an illegal fling, Sid."

"Yeah. I know. I kind of wish I'd thought about that now."

"I should have. I was, technically, the adult." Della put her hand on Sid's cheek. "But you were special. Half man, half boy."

"Della, I wouldn't be half the lover I am today if it hadn't been for you. I learned so much from you."

"I was only supposed to be teaching you algebra."

"Well, you know, Della, I am of age now. Unless your company has issues about consenting adults."

Della chuckled. "At least you've gotten a little more subtle than your hand up my skirt."

"I still remember the smell of your perfume."

"And I remember how sweet and how giving you were."

Sid moved in for a kiss, his hand sliding under the lapel of his jacket to remove the microphone hidden there. I checked my watch again. Nine-thirty.

"What's with that couple over there?"

I looked up at the man sitting on the stool next to me. He had that tall and gangly look, with darkish hair cut sort of short and dark horned-rim glasses. His eyes were dark and he was kind of cute. He was dressed in a suit and boring blue-striped tie, but the tie had been loosened and his collar was open. A plastic badge was clipped to his chest pocket, but I couldn't make out what it said.

"Oh," I said. "Um, that's my boss. I just work for him."

"I believe you," he said, glancing over at Sid and

Della, who were in full embrace and about to enact a porn movie if they stayed in the bar any longer.

"I shouldn't be so defensive," I sighed. "People see us together and assume we're sleeping together, and I just get tired of it, is all. I'm not that kind of girl."

"Really? What kind of girl are you?"

My grin got a little strained. "Religious." I stopped. "Sorry. I'm making a hash of this. I've never done the bar thing well, mostly because I don't do one night stands and every time I go into a bar, it seems like that's all anyone is interested in. Whatever happened to just having a good time being friends? I mean, I like dating. I just don't want to jump into bed with every guy I go out with."

My new friend laughed. "What a refreshing perspective. You know, I'm so tired of going on dates only to feel like I've got to perform or I'm some kind of mutant."

"You don't look like a mutant to me." I glanced over at the booth. Sid and Della had gone. "Looks like I'm off duty for the night."

"Hey, it's not late. My name's Fletcher Haddock. I'm here with the meeting. Um, I've got an extra ticket for the midnight show. Would you like to come with me?"

"Sure. That sounds like fun. I'm Lisa Wycherly."

"As in the sporting goods store over the state line?"

"Yeah. That's my parents' place, along with the resort. I can't believe it's so popular."

"Oh, yeah. We all know Wycherly's. It's a nice store."

"That's good to know." It certainly explained Della knowing it.

"Well, shall we?"

We had a lovely time. Fletcher and I had a lot in common, including the church thing. Not only was he a Catholic and still practicing, he even sang in his church's choir. We gambled a bit and Fletcher taught me how to play craps. You'd think growing up next to the casinos, I'd know these things. But one of the disadvantages of being a local kid in such a relatively small place as South Lake Tahoe is that the pit bosses knew us. In fact, I got carded that night by a boss who used to go to my old church.

The midnight show was entertaining. A comic named Gary Shandling was up first, then Juliet Prowse. Afterward, Fletcher walked me up to my room.

"I had a good time, Lisa," he said as we reached the door. He kept his arm tight across my shoulder.

"Me, too, Fletcher."

"You know, we don't have to end the evening now," Fletcher said, trying to sound casual and completely blowing it.

"Yeah, well, I do have to work tomorrow," I replied.

Fletcher moved in for a kiss. I was okay with that until I found myself all but choking on his tongue. And it was really wet, too. I pulled back.

"Um, Fletcher, I think I'm going to go to bed now."

"Why don't you let me come with you?" He grinned, but it wasn't working.

"No. I sleep alone. Remember? Thanks for a fun evening."

I slid into the room as fast as I could and all but slammed the door shut behind me.

Sid had, fortunately, shut the door to his bedroom, but I could still hear him and Della fully involved. Blushing and thoroughly disgusted, I went to my room and slammed the door. Either Sid got the hint or the door did its job. It didn't matter. The room was quiet and I went to bed.

September 16, 1983

The sound of a buzzer pulled me awake. Silence reigned. I looked at the room's clock radio. Three forty-one glowed back at me. The buzzer went off again, and I realized it was someone at the door of the suite. Yawning, I got my robe and went to answer it.

I wake up slow, and I really hate having my sleep interrupted, so maybe I was a little surly, to begin with.

"Yeah?" I grunted as I opened the door.

A short portly man in a badly cut suit flashed a badge at me.

"I'm Investigator Lehrer, Douglas County Sheriff's," he announced, walking in. "I'd like to ask you some questions."

"It's a quarter til four in the morning," I said.

"We've gotta get on this thing fast. You been here all evening?"

"I got in at one-thirty. Why?"

The coat closet door was open and Lehrer looked closely at Sid's overcoat.

"This your coat?" he demanded.

"No. It's my boss's."

"Where's he?"

"In his room, asleep."

"Has he been here all evening?"

"He was here when I got in. What is this all about?"

"Did you see him?"

"No, I heard him. Why are you here?"

"I'm investigating a crime, lady. Trot your boss out here. I gotta talk to him."

There didn't seem any point in antagonizing the jerk. I went over to the bedroom and rapped on the door.

"Sid? You want to wake up?"

I heard faint mumbling inside, but that didn't mean anything. Sid talks incessantly in his sleep.

"He's a very deep sleeper," I told Lehrer.

"So go in and wake him up."

I tried to remember if there was any due process that Lehrer was violating, but was too tired and fuzzy to think. The last thing I wanted to do was go into that bedroom. I knocked harder.

"Sid, wake up," I yelled. I turned to Lehrer. "I'm sorry. He's not going to wake up."

"Lady, go in and wake him. In the meantime, I'll have a little look around."

"Do you have a search warrant?"

"Not yet."

"Then wait until you do."

Taking a deep breath, I cracked the door and peeked in. Della had gone, but that wasn't the only reason I hesitated. Sid sleeps in the raw, and I wasn't interested in getting an education.

He was laying on his stomach on one side of the bed, with the blankets up to his shoulders. I went in and turned on the lights, leaving the door cracked open.

"Sid? Will you wake up?" I asked.

"It was worth it," he muttered, still out.

I went over and prodded his shoulder. "Come on, Sid, wake up."

He giggled. I shook him. "Sid, wake up."

I shook him again. It was no use. He was out cold. I debated pulling him out of bed and presenting him to Lehrer that way, but it would have humiliated Sid, not to mention me having to face him in his birthday suit.

I went into the bathroom and got a glass of water. In the bedroom, Sid rolled over onto his back. I sprinkled a few drops onto his chest.

"Try it again," he mumbled, not knowing what he was saying.

I did.

"Where is she? Where is she?"

I flicked water into his face. He grimaced, rubbed

at it, then slowly opened his eyes and sat up.

I turned my back quickly.

"Della?" he mumbled fuzzily.

"It's me, Lisa."

"I must have fallen asleep." He yawned, then sounded a lot more alert. "Why am I wet? And turn around. I'm covered."

And not one hair on his head was out of place. Even when he sleeps, it stays perfect.

I turned around. "I'm sorry. There's a sheriff's investigator out there who wants to talk to you. He insisted I wake you up." I put the glass of water on the nightstand.

"Cops?" He picked his pocket watch up off the nightstand and squinted at it. "It's almost four a.m. What the hell is he doing here?"

"I don't know. I asked, but he won't answer."

"Alright. Tell him I'll be out as soon as I get something on."

I nodded and left.

"He'll be out in a minute," I announced shutting the room.

"Lisa!" gasped a tall sandy-haired uniform officer.

Jimmy Roth had been one of the seven or so kids I mostly hung out with in high school. We'd lost touch shortly after graduation.

"Jimmy," I gasped back. "You're a cop?"

He rolled his eyes. "It's called making a living with a sociology degree. What are you doing here?"

"Shacking up," sniggered Lehrer.

"I'm sleeping in the other room," I snapped. Blushing, I looked at Jimmy. "I'm here with my boss."

"Why aren't you staying at your folks' place?"

"They're out of town."

Lehrer looked more closely at me. "You're local."

"Was," I said.

"Bill Wycherly's her dad," said Jimmy.

"Well, I'll be," muttered Lehrer.

Sid came out of the bedroom in a robe provided

by the hotel, and it was a safe bet, nothing else. It had probably taken him all that time to find it.

"What can I do for you?" he asked calmly.

"You Sid Hackbirn?" demanded Lehrer.

"Yes."

"Investigator Lehrer, Officer Roth, Douglas County Sheriff's Department. What time did you get back to your room tonight?"

"Roughly ten p.m."

"I understand you were not alone."

"No." Sid was acting completely bored.

"Who was she?"

Sid smiled. "I'm afraid I'm not at liberty to say."

"Real cute," Lehrer sneered. "I'm investigating a crime here."

"Obviously. Which crime?"

"The murder of Ms. Della Riordan."

I crossed myself. Sid stared at Lehrer.

"Della?" he whispered. "What happened?"

Completely satisfied, Lehrer read from his notebook. "At approximately two a.m., a room service waiter and some of the other guests heard a gun shot. The waiter saw someone leaving Ms. Riordan's room in a big hurry. The waiter investigated and found Ms. Riordan's body in her room. One of her co-workers, who had an adjacent room and also heard the shot, said Ms. Riordan accompanied you to this room around ten. That's why we're here."

Sid sank slowly onto the couch.

"You've confirmed the times," I said coolly. "Now will you please excuse us?"

"Not so fast," snapped Lehrer. "The suspect was wearing a tan overcoat, and I just happened to notice a tan overcoat hanging in that closet there. I'd like to look around here a little more closely."

"If a tan overcoat is the only probable cause you've got, then you're on very shaky ground," I growled, hanging onto my temper with both fists. "That overcoat has been hanging there since six thirty this evening.

As for searching the room, we will be happy to let you once we have been duly served with a search warrant."

"Listen, lady, I can make life plenty tough for you."

"That goes two ways, Investigator."

Lehrer glared at me, then left. Jimmy looked after him then back at me.

"Lisa," he said, worried. "It doesn't pay to get on Lehrer's bad side. He's a real S.O.B., and he plays tough."

"So do I, Jimmy."

Jimmy looked at me funny. "You've really changed, Lisa."

"In some ways. Haven't we all?"

"I'd better get going. Listen, uh, call me, huh? I just got married two months ago."

"Congratulations. Anyone I know?"

"Nah. A girl I met at Sacramento State." Jimmy swallowed. "You'd like her. See you."

He hurried out. Sighing, I turned to Sid, still sitting in shock on the sofa.

"Sid?" I asked softly.

He glanced at me, then shook his head.

"She's dead," he said quietly. "We made love. God, it was better than anything I remember, and..."

He swallowed. I sat down next to him and put my hand on his shoulder.

"Sid, go ahead and let your grief out. I'm here."

He looked at me and laid his hand on my knee.

"Thanks, but I'll be fine. I know you're just trying..." His voice broke, then he recovered. "Just trying to help, but I'll be okay. Really. I will."

"It'd be a shame if you didn't shed a few tears for the one woman you really loved."

He shook his head. "I don't cry, Lisa. I just don't." His eyes closed and he swallowed. "Oh, Christ, I just rolled over and fell asleep."

I put my arms around him and held him as the grief took over. His arms found their way around me and he laid his head on my shoulder. The tears came slowly and the sobs that shook him were silent. I kissed the soft, dark wavy hair.

"Let it out," I whispered softly and rocked him. "I'm here. Just let it out. It's alright."

It was a good long cry. Finally, Sid lifted his head from my shoulder. He sniffed once and wiped the tears from his face.

"I haven't cried since I was a small child," he said, embarrassed by the emotion.

"It's about time you did then."

"I don't know. It's such a shock." He paused. "They suspect me, don't they?"

"I wouldn't worry about it. I don't think Jimmy does, and Lehrer's just too taken with his own self-importance. I'm going to file a complaint tomorrow."

Sid took a deep breath. "We've also got some equipment to dispose of."

"That's right. All those guns we have won't look too good."

"We'll have to be very careful about how we sneak them out. We can't get caught with them on us. Damn it. I hate working unarmed."

"Let's not worry about it now. The courts don't open 'til ten, and the nearest one is in Carson City, I think. Lehrer won't be able to do anything until after that. We'd better get back to bed. It's been a long day, and sure as shooting, tomorrow will be just as long."

Sid yawned. "You mean today."

I got up and stretched. "Come on."

I pulled him up off the couch and pushed him to his room. He stopped at the door.

"Lisa, will you just hold me?"

I did. He shook ever so slightly, then rested. I almost didn't want him to let me go. When he did, he put his hand on my cheek.

"Lisa, I don't know what I'd do without you."

"I don't know what I'd do without you, Sid. Goodnight."

"Goodnight, Lisa."

I reached over and kissed his cheek, then went back to bed.

Sid let me sleep until seven thirty before banging on my door to get me to go running. Sid runs for an hour every morning and it's only on rare occasions that he lets me out of running with him. He was waiting for me when I finally stumbled out of my room in my warm up suit. I yawned and stretched.

"How are you feeling?" I asked softly.

"Better," he replied. "Fortunately, I've got other things to concentrate on. Let's get going."

His warm up suit looked pretty bulky, but I wasn't going to say anything.

"You know any place on the California side where we can run along the lakefront?" he asked as we went down the elevator.

"Not really. We could try the marina, but you don't really get any long stretches."

"Damn. I was hoping we could do this in California."

Downstairs, we found the Mercedes ourselves and drove up Highway 50 a ways further into Nevada. Sid parked near a stand of pines.

"I don't get it," I said, following him to the back of the car. "Where are we going to put everything?"

"In the car." He opened the trunk.

"But the search warrant will probably cover that, too."

Sid smiled. "That doesn't mean he'll find anything."

He felt for a minute under the rim.

"Got it." The floor of the trunk popped up. "Behold, my dearest ice maiden, a very good false bottom."

"That's pretty neat," I said smiling.

Sid double checked for passersby. There were none. He removed the warm up top. Underneath was all our equipment: two model thirteen revolvers with shoulder holsters, two twenty-two automatics with leg straps, lock picks, a miniature camera, two pairs of night binoculars, the transmitters and receivers, even a roll of silver duct tape.

"I left the strapping tape in your purse," said Sid handing it all to me. "And the viewer and the bug finder. We can explain those. Get this put away while I get my top back on. We don't want someone to see me like this."

"That and it's cold out here."

Our breath made little clouds, while in the sky, big clouds, some dark and threatening, floated across. Sid zipped up the front of his top and put his keys in his pocket.

"Don't worry," he said. "We won't run too long."

We were both a little tense as we stretched out. Neither of us is very fond of guns or using them. But being without them and on a job was pretty unnerving. We weren't completely unarmed. Both of us had a fair amount of equipment stashed in the soles of our shoes, and we both hid things in our hair, but it didn't have quite the same security firepower did.

There was also that pick up to check out. It was still in my purse. I had checked for it the night before and hadn't seen anything. That didn't mean it wasn't there. I hadn't looked very hard, and my purse is huge and things get lost in it. I figured Sid must have seen it when he got my gun and had decided that it wasn't anything suspicious. I decided to wait until he brought it up.

Back at the hotel, Sid called room service while I was in the shower. I know because the door buzzed just as I finished dressing and there was the waiter with breakfast. The tip was on the coffee table. The waiter put it all on the conference table and left with a smile on his face.

"Is that breakfast?" Sid called as I said grace in five seconds.

"Yep." I helped myself to fresh fruit salad.

"I'll be there in a minute. Do me a favor and don't start eating without me."

"Too late." I took advantage of Sid's absence to spread the butter extra thick on the whole wheat toast.

"Lisa, must you inhale everything within reach?"

"Not everything." I drained my glass of orange juice. "I'm leaving you your prune juice."

"Very funny."

"I thought so."

"Just leave me something to eat, will you?"

"Don't worry. I will. What I wouldn't do for a bowl of Lucky Charms right now."

The door to Sid's bedroom opened, and he stood in the doorway wearing a dark pinstriped three-piece suit with a white shirt and dark tie. The only thing marring his appearance was the look of utter disgust on his face.

"In the first place, Lisa, if you are going to make an offer like that, the least you could do is make it for something a lot more worthwhile, or at minimum, more palatable. In the second, must you turn my stomach so early in the morning?"

I shrugged and picked up my glass of milk. "Yuck! This is warm."

It was also non-fat, which I'll drink, but I don't like it.

"With all the fussing you do over waste, I'd think twice about leaving it."

I held my breath and swallowed. "This stuff is bad enough cold. Warm, it's positively vile."

I checked my watch. It was a little after nine. We had an appointment with the hotel manager at nine thirty.

Sid ate, completely distracted.

"You okay?" I asked.

"Fine," he replied, coming alert.

"Anything special you want to focus on during the meeting?"

He squeezed his eyes shut and rubbed his temple.

"I suppose I'd better start thinking about that."

"You want to reschedule it?"

"There's no point in it." He opened his eyes.

"Thinking about Della?"

"Yes and no. I'm thinking about that pickup. I can't help wondering if Della's murder isn't somehow connected to that job we're supposed to do." He got out his pocket watch and popped it open. A soft smile crept onto his lips as he checked the time to the quiet tinkling of the music box. "Why don't we go over the notes for the interview one more time? And remember, if you have any questions or ideas, I want you to make sure you ask."

"Right."

I was pretty nervous about the whole thing. Sid usually does his interviews by himself, although I get stuck transcribing the tapes. But this time was different. When the Tahoe job came up the week before, he mentioned that having a legitimate reason to be up there wouldn't be a bad idea. So we brainstormed out some article ideas, and I came up with one on how the casino was doing a lot to support arts and other community projects in the area. Sid really liked it, made a couple calls and had the article sold within an hour.

Then he insisted that I work on it, too, partly to make my presence more legitimate and partly because it was my idea, and well, I'd been doing some writing myself and was doing okay. [You were doing very well - SEH] Sid had been helping me a lot, but this was the first time we were technically collaborating.

I got out the file and the cassette recorder from my purse. I handed the file to Sid, then went rooting around for the batteries. Instead, I found an index card and a box about the same size wrapped in brown paper. I pulled them out.

"Sid, don't you think these look a little suspicious?"

He looked over at the box. "Where did that come from?"

"My purse. Didn't you see it when you got my gun this morning?"

"There are some things no man in his right mind will do, and one of them is examine the contents of a woman's purse. I grabbed the gun and got out." He took the card and box. "There's a cipher on this. Looks like you've got a meeting tonight. He says he can't afford to play guessing games, so it's got to be you. It's at one forty-five a.m. at a place called Road Show."

"Oh, help."

"You know it?" He tore the card into tiny pieces and stuck them in his pants pocket.

"Everybody knows the Road Show. No one would be caught dead there, but we all know it."

"What is it?"

"It's a bar down in Meyers, basically Tahoe's version of the wrong side of the tracks. A lot of truckers hang out there."

Sid grimaced. "Sounds lovely. Well, we'll have to table the logistics on this until later. We've got some interviews to do."

"What about the package? We can't leave it with Lehrer coming."

"We'll just have to find a place to hide it."

"But where?"

"For the moment, where you found it. We'll find someplace else as we go."

"Terrific." I put the box in my purse, my enthusiasm at a very low ebb.

Mr. Fred Jackson, the hotel manager, was middle-aged with sandy hair, a nice tan, and a trim figure. He greeted us congenially and made no objection to taping the interview.

"I just wish I could give you a little more time," he said. "Something came up with the office staff last night."

"Really? What?" asked Sid.

"Oh, nothing big. The cleaning staff is supposed to be out of here by ten at night, and they were goofing off again. It throws the security people off."

Sid mused. "Must be pretty tight up here."

Jackson chuckled. "Tight enough. But we're a lot more worried about all the cash downstairs. Mostly, the guards just have to wait for the cleaning staff to get out so they can lock up the offices. Listen, why don't you two make yourselves comfortable? Would you like some coffee? Tea? Mineral water?"

"Mineral water sounds good," said Sid. "Thank you."

"Miss Wycherly?"

I swallowed a yawn. "A cup of tea would be great. Thanks."

"Great. I'll be right back."

He left quickly. I took the box out of my purse and looked for a good place to hide it.

"Lisa, caffeine is a drug," Sid said, scowling as he dumped the pieces of the card he'd torn up into Jackson's waste basket.

"At the moment, I need it. I don't know how you're managing with so little sleep. Behind here?" I pointed to a small Native American statue on a shelf next to a window.

"Sure. Let's just hope Lehrer serves us quickly and we can get back here today." He turned out his pocket to be sure he'd gotten all of the torn-up pieces out.

"If we can't, I only saw a couple surveillance cameras, and they were pointed at the file cabinets."

"Let's keep an eye out for any others."

Jackson came back at that point, and we did our interview. It was close to ten thirty when Lehrer showed with the search warrant.

"Now hold on here, Carl," said Jackson. "I don't want you harassing my guests."

"I've got the warrant," said Lehrer. "Due process is being served. Come on, you two."

We went down to our suite. Two uniform cops, one a young woman, were already going through the sitting room.

"I want these two patted down," ordered Lehrer. He went into Sid's room.

"Okay, hands on your head," said the young man.

Bored, Sid did as he was told, and the young officer

went over him. The woman came up to me. I nervously put my hands on my head. Sid smiled at the woman.

"Aren't you going to pat me down?" he asked her, his eyes twinkling.

"Only on my own time," she replied with an amiable grin.

"You're clean," said the young man to Sid.

"What's your name?" Sid asked the young woman.

"Marcia Alwitz."

Lehrer came back into the sitting room. "You two take the room apart. I want to look at his car."

"I'll take you down," said Sid. He winked at Marcia. "Let me know when you're off."

She chuckled, then went over me quickly.

"Doesn't that bother you?" she asked as she finished. "Purse."

I handed it to her. "What?"

"Him picking up on me like that. I mean, I know he was only joking."

"Oh, he was serious."

Shaking her head, Marcia emptied the purse out onto the conference table.

"Sheez. If my boyfriend did that to me, I'd drop him on his can so fast his eyeballs'd spin right out of their sockets."

Her partner laughed. "That's if he was lucky."

I checked the name on his badge. It was Shockney.

"He's not my boyfriend," I sighed. "I just work for him."

"That's not what Lehrer says," snickered Shockney.

"Hey," growled Marcia. "It's bad enough the guy's suspected of murder."

"He didn't do it," I said. "He loved Della."

"Don't worry," said Marcia. "Lehrer's just got some ax to grind is all. They haven't got a thing on your boss. The waiter said the suspect was tall and dressed real ratty."

"Great, Marcia," said Shockney. "Discuss the case with the suspects."

"Have you found anything?" she returned. "Do you honestly think we're going to?"

She had her hand on my bug finder, only it looks like a beeper, so she paid it no mind. Shockney tossed a pillow back onto the couch.

"This is pointless," he grumbled and went into my room.

Marcia swept all my stuff back into my purse. A few minutes later, Lehrer and Sid returned. Lehrer was not happy.

"Find anything on her?" he snarled at Marcia.

"'Fraid not, sir," she replied.

"Where's Shockney?"

Marcia pointed. Lehrer went into my room. Marcia smiled at Sid.

"I'm told you weren't joking," she said.

"I do and I don't," he said, his smile lecherous.

"Sid, must you?" I groaned.

He sighed, then smiled at Marcia. "We'll talk later."

Lehrer stomped out of my room grumbling. He glared at Sid and me.

"You're clean. I don't know how the hell you did it, but you're clean."

"It might be because we didn't do anything," said Sid.

"You're not off the hook yet," said Lehrer. "And I'd watch the smart remarks, Hackbirn. You'll only make trouble for yourself."

He nodded at Shockney and Marcia, and they left. Sid took a deep breath in the silence that followed. He pulled his pocket watch out and popped it open. The tinkling of Bach's Minuet in G slowly eased the tension in the room. He smiled softly, letting it play, then popped it shut.

"We've got just enough time to make our next interview," he said. "Let's go."

We spent the rest of the morning interviewing the president of the Lake Tahoe Cultural Arts Alliance, then various other civic group leaders. All of them knew my parents, and several knew me.

"What I want to know, Lisa," asked my old drama teacher, who also ran the community theater company, "is what is all this nonsense I'm hearing about you and that murder in Stateline last night?"

I looked over at Sid. He shifted but remained calm.

"It's a long story," I said. "Sid and I really didn't have anything to do with it. It was just bad luck that the victim was... Well, she and Sid had been visiting."

Mrs. Roberts gave Sid the once over and smiled. "Oh."

"Why don't we start with how the casino has been helping your group?" said Sid.

That, more or less, kept her distracted, and the subject didn't come up again.

We tried meeting up with Mr. Jackson at the hotel around one, but he swept us out of his office and took us to lunch in his private dining room. After we finished eating, Jackson shook our hands and explained he had other business and went running off. We went back to the suite.

"Just great," grumbled Sid.

"I guess we'll just have to break in and get the box," I said.

"Yeah. That's only one more thing to worry about."

"We've got it pretty well staked out. It shouldn't be too bad, and I brought my break in pants."

"But there's always that element of risk, and on top of that, there's that dive where the meeting is."

"Now that's going to be problematic. I'm going to have to drive there, but if you still want your Mercedes, I don't recommend parking it in that lot."

"Is it that rough?" Sid frowned, and I wasn't sure if he was more worried about me or his car. [You could defend yourself, the Mercedes couldn't - SEH]

I shrugged. "It is, in a way. It's a dirt parking lot, and with the rain we've had, it's probably mud now. And the clientele, if they don't drive eighteen wheelers, they drive four by four's. A slick foreign machine like that four fifty SL is just begging to get hit."

"And even if it wasn't, it would undoubtedly attract attention. Why don't you rent a car?"

I shook my head. "Why would I? I have yours, and we've been driving all over the place, so there's no way I could say we don't. Even if they don't recognize me at the rental place, they know my name."

"Which has been all over the place with Della's murder." Sid paced. "But where are we going to get a second set of wheels?"

"I'd suggest saying your car isn't starting, but then everyone would wonder why we don't take it to one of the local garages. They're already wondering why I'm not staying at my folks' place as it is. Wait." I sat up and got my keys out of my purse. "I am, at long last, vindicated."

"What?" Sid looked at me.

I jangled the fully loaded ring at him. "You have made your final cut on all my keys. On this ring are the keys to my parents' store, house, garage, truck, and jeep, namely, our second set of wheels."

"Wouldn't people recognize your parents' cars?"

"Not necessarily." I grinned. "There must a couple hundred white jeeps in this valley alone. And it's got to be there. Mama and Daddy flew out according to Mae."

Sid mused. "Can you get it without anyone knowing?"

"No sweat. Neff and Mary are the closest neighbors, and they live on the other side of the horse barns. One of the guests might hear something, but I doubt they'd do anything, and the house is set a good ways off from them anyway."

"I guess you're on then." Sid paced. "I'll help you break into the office, but then you'll have to go the rest of the way by yourself."

"Why don't I just pull the break in by myself? If you're there, it's just another person to get caught."

"I suppose. I'll take care of getting your guns and

the lockpicks. I don't want you unarmed."

I sighed.

"I know you don't like it," said Sid. "But I don't want anything to happen to you, Lisa. You be very careful."

"You be careful, too. I don't want to end up filing for unemployment again."

Sid smiled at me. "You'll never have to worry about that again."

"I suppose the business can keep me, but I'll have to find some sort of visible job. I can't very well work for you if you're dead."

Sid started pacing again.

"I'm sorry," I said. "I didn't mean to be so blunt. I know you don't like thinking about it."

"I have to occasionally." He stopped and sat down next to me. "Lisa, if something happens to me, I've seen to it that you will be provided for, so you'll never have to worry about unemployment or a visible job again."

I got up. "Sid, I was just joking. What I meant was that I care about you and that I don't want to see anything happen to you. So, don't go and do something silly."

"A- It's not something silly. I've got to leave it to somebody, and B-..." He looked away. "It's already done. It's been done for a long time. You're not getting all of it. I've got a couple charities and a friend or two, and you will be required to pay for educating your sister's kids so they won't have to worry. But you are the primary beneficiary."

"I don't want to be, Sid."

"Well, you are. Admittedly, it's not until after I'm gone."

"I don't want it. Sid, if something happened to you, I'd be crushed. But I don't want your will hanging over me while you're alive. I appreciate the thought, really, I do. I just don't feel right taking your money."

"Who else am I going to leave it to? I don't have any relatives."

"What about your aunt?"

"Stella? Hell, no. I'm not going to leave my money to someone who A- doesn't need it because I found out she received a similar bequest, B- never wanted me in the first place, C- absolutely refuses to see or talk to me; you wouldn't believe what a time I had just getting her lawyer to let me know when she dies; and D- could very well die before I do anyway, our business notwithstanding." Sid got up and laid his hand on my shoulder. "Lisa, I'm not saying you should be dancing on my grave. But if you'll excuse the Republican attitude, if you don't get it, the government will, and they're already taking too much now, not to mention the chunk they'll take when you do get it. Besides, you're the only person I've ever really been close to. Even Della, who got closer than anyone, wasn't as close to me as you are. I care about you tremendously. Things happen too easily in our business. I don't want to see you left out in the cold, especially when you could be comfortable."

I flopped onto the couch. "You don't understand, Sid. I don't want to be a kept woman. If I'm going to have a fortune, I want to earn it myself."

"I didn't earn mine."

"Maybe when the time comes, I'll feel differently. Right now, I feel like I'm taking advantage of you."

He smiled softly. "Sometimes I wish you would."

"Are you insinuating again?"

"No." Mischief lit up his face. "But I could."

Relieved that the more serious moment had passed, I decided to try something I'd been thinking about doing for some time.

"You could try sitting next to me," I suggested coyly, or what I hoped was coyly.

"Why?" Sid was suspicious, and well he should have been. But he walked over.

"Because."

"This is not a come on."

"Never."

"And you say you don't believe in teasing."

"It depends on what kind."

"So, what do you want?"

"A little something." I patted the couch next to me.

He sat down really close. "Maybe a little something that I promise will go no further."

He moved in, his head tilted, his lips just barely parted.

"Maybe not!" I yelled, messing up his hair.

Sid bounced back. "What? What the hell did you just do?"

He got up and went straight for the mirror. "Lisa, what in heaven's name is this? I don't get it. Where's my brush, damn it."

"Here, use mine." I got my vent brush out of my purse and tossed it to him.

He caught it, looking at me like a wounded puppy.

"Are you mad at me?" I asked, suddenly uncertain.

He slid his little piece of spring steel out, then brushed everything into place.

"No," he said finally. He tossed the brush back to me and replaced the steel, with a sneaky little smile. "I don't get mad. I get even."

I nodded and got up. "I think I'll take a nap."

I went to my room, making sure I had all my personal belongings in there with me and bolted the door. Sid's ability with locks is such that it was technically pointless, but I was hoping he'd respect the gesture.

I woke up around five, really hungry. [The sound you hear is me biting my tongue - SEH] After putting on some jeans and a sweater and grabbing my purse, I went into the sitting room to look for Sid. I found him in front of the door to the suite, necking with some woman I'd never seen before. At least they were dressed.

"Uh, Sid?" I asked.

She jumped and yelped. Sid, the slob, took it all in stride.

"Hello, Lisa," he said smiling. "This is Doreen. Doreen, Lisa, my secretary."

"Nice to meet you," I said.

"Same," said Doreen, still recovering from her shock.

"Is there anything you need, Lisa?" asked Sid.

"Yeah. Dinner."

Sid bit his tongue. We have an agreement that we don't make fun of each other in front of his girlfriends.

"Um, I'm sorry, but I wasn't sure when you were getting up, and..." He glanced at Doreen.

"I'll go by myself," I said, then nodded at the door and Sid and Doreen in front of it. "If you guys will just excuse me."

"Oh." Sid gently escorted Doreen out of the way. "By all means. Excuse us."

I couldn't help being disgusted by Sid's super smooth persona, but I had to admit it was one of the things I had originally liked about him. I guess I knew him too well to buy it anymore.

There's a coffee shop next door to the hotel that offers dirt cheap meals in the hopes that patrons will leave lots of change in their slot machines. I paid for the more expensive chili burger, partly because I love them and partly because I wanted to get Sid back.

I had just tucked in when Fletcher Haddock slid into the booth across from me.

"I've been looking for you all day," he said.

"I've been working."

"Well, of course. Look, I want to apologize for last night."

I didn't answer.

"I understand if you don't want to talk to me anymore," he continued, just this side of pathetic. "I really am a nice guy. You know how these places can get to you. I really wasn't going to try anything."

I shook my head. "Fletcher, do we have to go through this B.S.?"

"I'm serious. I'm not trying to put the moves on you."

"You know, if I had a dime for every time I've

heard that line from a guy, I'd have more money than my boss." I glared at him. "Did it ever occur to you guys that you might get a little respect if you were just upfront about the whole thing? You're not going to get any, anyway."

Fletcher got out a business card from his sports jacket.

"I'd like to start over again," he said, scribbling on the back. "That's my home phone on the back. If you ever want to just talk. Maybe you're in trouble or something. Give me a call."

He put the card next to my plate. I glared at it. But inside, I was puzzled. Why had he said that bit about being in trouble? He left. I put the card in my purse.

I slummed around the casino for a bit, but I knew I was going to have to go back to the room and change for the break in. I got there around eight, and the radio was on in the other room. I turned on the TV in my bedroom and turned it up loud.

I don't know what time Doreen left. Sid knocked on my door at eleven thirty and helped me get together everything I needed for the break in. I wore the special black pants I'd made with lots of extra pockets, which carried the case of lock picks and a miniature flashlight, and a long sleeved white shirt, with a dark ski jacket. I also had on my shoulder holster and my twenty-two strapped to my shin. In the pockets of my jacket were black kid leather gloves, a dark all over ski mask, and my key ring. My feet were clad in my armored running shoes, the ones with all sorts of goodies hidden in the soles.

"Go get 'em," said Sid as I opened the suite door.

He paused for a second, then lightly punched my arm.

Sliding around the view of the surveillance cameras was more nerve-wracking than difficult. Getting the door to Mr. Jackson's office open was not easy, but then I'm not that good with locks. I slid in and found the room faintly lit by the lights outside. The little box was right where I'd left it. I stashed it in my pants and left.

I got the Mercedes out of the parking lot and headed for California. The streets were still pretty crowded, which wasn't surprising. I checked for a tail and found none.

It only took a few minutes to get to my parents' resort. I parked the Mercedes in a dark corner of the guest lot, next to the creek. I circled around the horse barn, keeping my distance. The horses still nickered and raised a mild fuss, the sort we usually blamed on cats. I had to pass pretty close to several guest cabins. A late arrival in number three was just bedding down. Number one had a party going, with people spilling out the door. I made another wide circle. The moment I stepped into my parents' yard, Murbles and Richmond, my parents' two over-sized mutts started barking like crazy. I slid to the front door.

"Murbles, Richmond, quiet!" I commanded.

They yipped and whined, and I could hear them sniffing at the door. I went over to the garage, digging out my keys. It took a minute to find the padlock key, and by that time, I could see two flashlights coming my way. I ran back to the house.

Murbles and Richmond started up again as I unlocked the door. I slid in and got pounced on. They were delighted to see me.

"Down!" I hissed. "Shut up! Quiet."

They quieted. I scratched their heads trying to listen out front. It was Neff and Mary, alright. They're the elderly couple who have been caretaking for my parents since they first bought the place. Daddy's offered them retirement, but they keep saying no. They prefer working.

"What do you think, Neff?" Mary's voice asked.

A flashlight's beam passed across the front windows.

"The dogs are quiet. I don't see any sign of a break-in," said Neff. "It was probably one of those kids in number one."

"But the horses were spooked. I think we ought to check inside."

"What for? Nobody's gotten in that I can see. You're just being skittish, honey."

"I don't mean to be, but with all that trouble in Nevada."

"That can be explained."

"I just don't understand..."

Their voices faded out as they returned to their place. I waited, disgusted. It figured Mary would have heard the dogs. She's a nervous woman to begin with, which is why I usually avoid her and Neff. She always makes me feel like I'm about to break something, and complains constantly when I'm around. Of course, when I don't make a point of visiting her right away, she acts hurt until I do.

I waited about ten minutes before leaving the house. It was getting very close to one fifteen, which didn't leave much time for getting down to Meyers. I got the garage open, and let the jeep roll down the drive. I had originally planned on starting the jeep in the garage to make sure it was running, but I didn't want Mary getting her back up again. After closing the garage door, I tried the engine. It roared to life without a problem.

I have to admit, my mouth was dry and my hands were all but shaking as I pulled up to the Road Show. In other communities, kids terrorize each other with haunted houses. With all the gold mining ghosts, those were no big deal to us. We had the Road Show for horror stories, and there was no doubt that it was real.

It looks like any roadside dive you've ever seen, with a cheap white lighted sign in front, and big rigs and four by fours in the lot. There may be a sedan or two, but you can bet they're American made or they don't have windows.

I found a straw cowboy hat in the backseat of the jeep and put it on, pulling the brim down over my face.

Inside, was dim, with red lights, and noisy and filled with cigarette smoke. Two heavy guys wearing flannel plaid shirts were playing pool, the cracks in their behinds showing every time they bent over for a shot. What few women were there wore western shirts open to expose their cleavage and tight jeans. The men wore their toughness like a red flag. I caught more than a few furtive, calculating stares.

They were mostly white with a few Hispanics, so I was surprised when my arm was tapped by a young black man, also in a flannel shirt and jeans. He was also the bartender in the Keno Lounge.

"Out back," he muttered at me and went to the bar.

I looked around once more, then left and headed around to behind the building, stepping over another flannel-shirted man face down in the mud. A friend of his groaned and wretched.

The bartender was waiting for me.

"You Little Red?" he asked.

"Yeah."

"Tom Collins, Division 11B." Which was a CIA division.

I swallowed. "Why aren't you overseas?"

He chuckled. "You got need to know on this?"

"No," I sighed.

"It's a domestic division. We coordinate with our overseas operatives when something starts over there and winds up here."

"Then why are we being pulled in?"

"I may have been spotted."

I nodded. "That's what we heard. What's going down?"

"There's an enemy transponder up here. Somebody, probably local, is getting in secrets from the Bay area and uploading the info to a Soviet spy satellite. The problem is that the signal is real random and the transponder is mobile, so we can't pin it down. He's getting the stuff in through some hired help, and we figured we could use the recreation goods group that's meeting here this weekend as cover. That's why you're here now."

"Let me guess. Our job is to flush the sender and his people out."

"Exactly. We've tracked the secrets to Sunland Products."

"Oh, my god. The murder."

"Yeah, it may not have been so coincidental. Which means we need to know who killed Della Riordan and why. And it gets better. The transponder was ours."

"Oh. So someone's selling out."

"Was selling out. We got her, just not before she'd passed the transponder and a bunch of other equipment on. We just don't know to who, just that it was up in this area."

"Great. So, what do you want done with the box you dropped last night?"

He looked at me. "What box?"

"The box I found in my purse with the card."

"I just dropped the card."

"I see." About as well as Stevie Wonder. "Alright. You got anything else for us?"

"Not at the moment. You can make contact with me at the Keno Lounge."

"It'll have to be code two. This job's going to be tricky enough, with me being a local."

He gaped. "What?"

"I grew up here. Someone up top goofed, either that or they figured my nice girl image would cover up a lot. You said an operative no one will begin to suspect."

"That stinks." [Is that really what he said? - SEH] "Alright. We'll avoid contact as much as possible, and I'm stepping out of the picture completely."

"Fine. Um. Later."

I went back to the parking lot. The bar was just emptying, and not a few of the patrons were fighting with each other. It was tricky getting the jeep out of the lot and up the highway in one piece around all those drunks, but I did and replaced it in my parents' garage without trouble. The dogs started barking again, but the party in number one was still going, so Neff and Mary didn't show.

The radio was going in the other room when I let myself back into the suite. The coat closet was open, too, and next to Sid's overcoat hung a green bomber jacket with a patch on the shoulder that read Douglas County Sheriff's Deputy.

September 17, 1983

If Sid slept in the next morning, he wasn't about to let me know it. He got me to go running at seven again. We went to the lakefront and hid lockpicks and guns in the trunk of the car. I told him over breakfast what had happened the night before.

"Essentially," I said as I finished. "It all went as smooth as silk."

He nodded. "I figured it would. After all, I trained you."

"Very funny."

"I thought so."

"You won't think this is." I went over to my ski jacket and pulled out the box. "It wasn't part of the pickup."

"Then where did it come from?"

"Good question." I tossed it to him.

He opened one end and pulled out a sealed plastic bag filled with white powder.

"Let me guess," I said. "That's some illegal substance?"

"I'd say that's as good a guess as any." Sid got up and paced.

"Aren't you supposed to dip your finger in and taste it?"

Sid laughed. "Are you kidding? Who knows what that stuff is laced with? It could even be straight poison like cyanide or something. Just a taste of that'd have me pining for the fjords in no time." He paused, thinking. "I wonder if I brought it."

He went to his room.

"What?" I asked following him into the bathroom.

"Henry got me a chemical analysis kit a couple years ago when I had a case with a lot of different substances floating around. I put some fresh test chemicals in my kit last July before I went to the Bahamas.”

“Sounds like some interesting parties.”

“Not that trip.” Sid got the leather kit off the counter and opened it. “And they are still here.”

He pulled out the little sample bottles labeled shampoo, conditioner, hand lotion, and a couple others.

“I need some more glasses,” he said, unwrapping the three on the counter.

I got two more off the dresser in the bedroom.

Sid filled each with a different clear liquid and put the corresponding bottle next to the glass.

“Are we ready?” he asked, with a mischievous grin.

“Go for it,” I said.

The first glass clouded up, then cleared, leaving a tiny bit of residue on the bottom. Sid shook his head and dropped some powder into the next glass. The liquid turned bright blue in a second.

“Woh. That’s coke.”

“Cocaine?” I asked.

“Very pure cocaine.” He looked at the first glass. “This precipitate is probably just talcum powder. Must have been cut only once.” He picked up the bag. “Want a snort?”

I pulled back. “I hope you’re joking.”

“Mostly.” He looked at the bag. “It’s one hell of a high. I got a hold of a couple lines when I first got to ‘Nam, and nearly got myself killed as a result. It was just too dangerous for someone doing intelligence work. I decided I liked staying alive more.”

“You did drugs?”

“Some. Mostly the occasional joint to be part of the crowd. But I’d been around it all my life and knew too many people who were dying from it to be really interested.”

Sid’s Aunt Stella, who raised him, was a Communist, and he grew up with a bunch of radicals and hippies before they were called hippies, which is why he doesn't see anything wrong with free love. He was taught that it was normal and natural, and that's all.

I wandered back into the sitting room. "It just seems so weird that your brain isn't fried. I know a girl from high school who's so out of it, and it had to be drugs. She wasn't like that in school."

"That's why I wasn't interested." Sid followed me out.

I noticed some papers on the coffee table. "What are these?"

"Autopsy report on Della."

"That fast?"

"Not a lot of corpses in Douglas County."

I picked the report up. "Where did you get it?"

"Marcia asked me if I wanted it, and I said yes, and she brought it up last night. She thought there might be some morbid curiosity, which at that point it was."

"Three fifty-seven, three shots to the chest," I read aloud. "Had recently had sexual intercourse, probably more than once. How many times did you two do it?"

Sid winced. "Only twice. I'm afraid I'm not seventeen anymore."

My face felt hot. "I had to ask." I turned back to the report. "Shots were at close range, but no other signs of a struggle. That's odd."

"Not if she knew her killer. There weren't any signs of a struggle in her room either."

I looked over the report. "It doesn't say anything about the room."

"I searched it this morning. It was clean. However, an interesting point, a pro had gone over it before me."

"Tom Collins. No, it can't have been him. He would have said something last night, and I'm certain he intends to stay out of this."

Sid just shrugged.

"So how are we going to find the killer?" I asked.

"We could try asking the Sunland people."

I sighed. "I'm sure they'll tell us a lot."

"If we ask the right questions, probably more than they want to. They're all in their meeting right now. Why don't I try later?"

I picked up my purse. "Sure. For now, I think I'll take a walk. I've been wanting to since I got here."

"Fine with me. Just take care of yourself."

His smile was soft and gentle. I smiled back and beat it out of there in a hurry.

There's a little clearing near the Heavenly ski area that I call my "by myself" place. Murray Waters, the manager at my father's store, showed it to me the summer I was sixteen. Murray and I weren't really close or anything like that. He'd just caught me sobbing in the stockroom over the usual adolescent woes, and showed me his favorite place to go when he was bugged. It was his way of reaching out.

It took me an hour to hike there. It's surrounded by tall pines, except on one side, where a huge boulder forms a flat table overlooking the valley. The granite was rough and sparkled in the morning sun, and was freezing cold to the touch. I only spent a few minutes breathing in the still, then checked my watch and hiked back into town.

As I passed Daddy's store, I stopped short. It was closed. I looked at my watch. Eight minutes after eleven. Even on Saturday mornings, as it was, the store opened at nine on the dot. Only on Sundays did the store open at eleven. It wasn't like Murray to be that irresponsible.

Puzzled and frowning, I went around to the back. It was locked, too. I hefted out my key ring and unlocked the door.

"Hello?" I called, stepping into the dark stockroom.

No answer. I shut the door and turned on the light.

"Anybody here? Murray?"

I stepped through the shelves. The place was deserted. Near the door to the front of the store was a small desk attached to the wall. Above it was the wall phone, and next to the phone was a yellowed sheet of paper with names and phone numbers on it. It was so old, my name was still on it, from when I worked there in high school and during the summers when I was in college.

Murray's number had been crossed out and had a new number next to it. I dialed the new number. No answer. I tried the old number, but that had been disconnected. On the list, several names had been crossed out and a couple news ones added. There was one name that I knew, Rita Hodges. She's worked part time there ever since I can remember. I called her.

"Rita?" I asked when she answered. "This is Lisa Wycherly."

"Lisa. I heard you were back in town."

"Yeah, it's business. I'm at the store right now, and it hasn't been opened."

"Where's Murray?"

"I haven't the faintest. I called him, but got no answer."

"Oh dear. That's just not like Murray. I guess I'd better come in. Just give me a few minutes to turn the roast off. Oh dear. I hope my kids haven't left yet. They were coming over today."

The guilt got me. Sid usually lets me have my weekends to myself. The meeting wasn't due to let out until later that evening, anyway, and Sid had more or less said he was going to take care of talking to the Sunland people.

"Rita, don't worry. I'll work it. I've still got the keys. They haven't made any big changes, have they?"

"Well, there's that new computerized register."

I looked into the store. "That one. I was still here when they put it in. Do you know who's working tomorrow? I don't see the schedule."

"It's on the back of the door like usual, and I always do open to close on Sundays."

"That's right. Great. It'll give me some time to find Murray. I'll talk to you later."

"Bye-bye, Lisa."

I hung up, then turned on the lights and went through the store. Everything was in perfect shape and ready to open. Even the stock room had been straightened. There was one shelf next to the desk that was pretty sloppy, with boxes upside down and skewed, but that certainly wasn't anything unusual. Several cardboard cases were scattered among the shelves waiting to be unpacked, nothing strange about that. The store safe still had the previous night's deposit bag, which was a little odd. The change bag for the register drawer was as it was supposed to be. I counted it out: one hundred and fifty dollars down to the penny.

I shut the register drawer, took a deep breath, unlocked the front door and turned around the closed sign. There were only a few people on the street, pretty much as could be expected for that time of year. I called Sid from the stockroom phone, leaning in the doorway. A couple wandered in and browsed.

"Hello?" asked Sid's voice. It had a thick, funny feel to it. I figured he was asleep, although now that I think about it, I should have known better.

"It's me. Something's come up-"

"Mm. Is it urgent?"

"Well... I don't know."

"Can it wait an hour or two?"

"I suppose."

"Oh, honey, watch the teeth!" This was obviously not directed at me, but it startled the heck out of me nonetheless. "That's better, much better, oh yes."

My face flushed red hot. "Um, you're not alone, are you?"

"Not at all." He chortled, then let out a happy sigh. "Is there a number where I can call you?"

I gave it to him and we hung up. I didn't get much chance to grumble about it. The couple decided they wanted to buy some postcards, and three teenage girls walked in. It continued just busy enough to keep me from wondering about Sid until around one fifteen. He called about two minutes later, just as I located the work schedule taped to the back side of the stockroom door.

"Sorry about taking so long to get back to you," he said, his voice back to normal. "She's not taking off."

"Oh. But..."

"She's in the shower. What's up?"

"I'm at my parents' store. The guy that runs it isn't here. I dropped by at eleven, and the store was still closed, and there's no trace of Murray. I figure I may as well take over for the moment."

"Given what's been going on, something feels funny about that."

"The same thought crossed my mind. But nothing's messed up here. I gave the store a good once over before I opened. There is another possible explanation. Murray's always been very trustworthy, but there've been an awful lot of rumors that he has a gambling problem, and I've gotten just enough hints from him to believe it might be true. Something could have pushed him over the deep end and he took off."

"That's just plausible enough that we can't overlook it. How long do you think you'll be there?"

"Good question." I looked at the schedule. An Alice Martin was scheduled to show at two. "We've got a girl coming in, but I'm going to have to give her a break before I leave."

"I suppose you should."

A young man wandered up to the counter with a pan for gold kit and two souvenir mugs. I propped the phone against my shoulder and rung him up.

"That is, of course, assuming the girl shows. That'll be twenty-three twenty- seven," I told my customer.

"Why wouldn't she?" asked Sid as I made change.

"Have a nice day," I said to the young man. "I have no idea. Just the way things are going at the moment."

Sid chuckled. "You may have a point. Why don't I meet you down there?"

"Sure. Can you bring me some food? We've got

nothing here but trail mix, and I've missed lunch."

"Given your appetite, that's tantamount to a catastrophe. I'll see what I can do."

"I can't wait," I grumbled blandly. "I'll talk to you later."

I hung up, pondering Alice Martin. The name sounded vaguely familiar. Then it hit. My girlfriend, Leslie Bowman, had babysat for the Martins when we were in high school. She'd always complained about how unreliable the parents were, always coming home hours later than they said they would, and what a precocious brat the little girl, Alice, was. I did some figuring and realized Alice had to be around sixteen.

It seemed strange that Murray would hire someone so young, but there seemed to be a lot of strangeness surrounding Murray at that moment. I checked the schedule again. Both Alice and Ruth were almost working full time for the next two weeks. That made sense, especially with those cases in the stockroom. It was time for winter changeover when all the summer sporting goods were packed away and the winter stuff put out. It was a royal pain, too. I decided that the front needed watching more than the cases needed unpacking.

I did go ahead and call the hospital, hoping to find Murray. He wasn't there, and the nurse I talked to not only knew him but said that no unidentified patients had been admitted either. I called the police. They went over and checked his place. His car was there, but he wasn't. The officers said there wasn't anything they could do until he'd been missing seventy-two hours or I had good reason to suspect foul play. I did, but my reasons were too closely linked to Quickline, so I let it go.

By the time two o'clock rolled around, Sid still hadn't shown. Neither had Alice. Around two twenty, I was helping a customer dig out some blueberry muffin mix from among the trail food when the door banged open with a loud jangle.

"Murray!" bellowed the youthful female voice. "Murray, I've got a big problem. I've got to take Friday off. You've gotta let me have it."

"Excuse me," I told my customer, then went over to the counter. "Murray's not here. You must be Alice."

She stepped back. She was blonde with long full hair that had been feathered back from her face and glued in place with hair spray. Her eyes were blue and framed with too much mascara. Tight jeans emphasized her round, but slender seat, while a tight, low cut v-necked sweater made the most of her ample chest.

"Who are you?" she demanded as I went to the register to ring up the customer.

"Hold on," I said, then rang up the muffin mix.

Alice waited impatiently while I gave the guy his change.

"Who do you think you are?" she exploded as soon as the customer had left. "You can't just walk in here and work like you own the place."

"But I do, more or less. I'm Lisa Wycherly."

"Oh. Like he's your dad or something?"

"He's my father."

"Awesome." She thought that one over with both brain cells. "Where's Murray?"

I shrugged. "I was hoping you'd know."

"Fat chance. You knew about the divorce."

"I'd heard something about it."

"Darla totally wiped him out. She, like, got everything, the house, the kids, the furniture, his dogs even, except for one."

"How sad." Somewhere in the back of my mind it registered that Murray and Darla were dog breeders, or had been.

"He's totally broken up about it."

"Maybe that has something to do with why he's not here."

Alice gaped. "Oh man, you don't mean, like, he might have killed himself or something?"

"Let's hope it was the something. In the meantime, there's not much we can do about it."

"But what am I going to do about Friday?"

"We'll see. Maybe Rita can work it. You'll have to talk to her, though. I'm not even supposed to be here. Why don't you watch the front while I get some of that stock put away?"

Moping, Alice dumped her purse under the register and slumped onto the stool behind the counter. I checked my watch. There was no telling when Sid was going to show.

"Alice, I'm going to go get something to eat," I said, picking up my purse. "I'm expecting my boss to come by. When he gets here, will you ask him to wait, please?"

"Is he single and cute?"

"He's over eighteen, and you're not."

"What makes you so sure?" She smirked.

She did look older than she was.

"Remember your old babysitter, Leslie?"

"Yeah."

"She was my best friend. She told me all about that time you and your cousin stayed up after you were supposed to be in bed and did nude cheesecake poses for each other."

Alice groaned in pure adolescent agony. Smirking myself, I tossed my purse over my shoulder and went in search of lunch. I got a double burger, chili fries and black cherry malted to go from a hamburger stand down the street.

I returned to the store through the back and shut the door quietly. Neither Sid nor Alice noticed my entrance. They stood in the doorway to the front of the store, Alice leaning casually against the doorjamb, with Sid leaning on a hand placed above her and moving in for a kiss.

"She's jailbait, Sid," I said loudly.

Still smooth, Sid pulled back, chuckling and shaking his finger at her.

"Nice try, little girl," he said.

Alice shifted her chest. "Maybe she's, like, jealous."

"Really?" replied Sid, with a bemused grin. "You got the I.D. to prove it?"

"Yeah." Alice went after her purse.

"Trust me, Sid," I said. "She is, without a doubt, a minor."

Sid chuckled. "No fooling. She looks like she could be old enough, but I was going to card her."

"Here," said Alice, putting the card in Sid's face.

Still smiling, Sid examined the surface, then held it up to the light. He laughed.

"Where'd you buy this?" he chuckled, handing it back.

"Reno," said Alice in a small voice. "My friend got it for me."

"Tell your friend to find a forger with the right paper," said Sid.

"Well, I'm still eighteen."

"Then why give me a phony I.D.?" Sid shook his head. "I'm sorry, honey, but I'm afraid not."

"Come on. Why not?"

"When an overage guy plays with an underage girl, if they get caught, much anguish ensues."

"That's if they get caught." Alice presented her chest again. "I'm not, like, telling anyone."

Sid smiled. "There'll be nothing to tell. Like my good friend said, you're jailbait, honey, and frankly, I'm not looking to get busted. After you're eighteen, I'm all yours. Until then, them's the breaks. I'm sorry."

Moping, Alice slumped off into the front.

"You don't know how sorry," Sid muttered, then turned to me.

"You can quit drooling now," I snipped, dumping my lunch on the little desk. I looked at him. "I'm sorry. I shouldn't be such a grouch. This whole thing with Murray has got me bugged. I was going through the stock out front to find out what we had so I could help the customers. We've got a lot of Sunland Products in."

I opened the bag.

"I have a very nice tuna sandwich for you," said Sid.

"Thanks. Why don't you put it in the fridge there? I'll eat it later." I spread out the paper the hamburger had been wrapped in and put the carton of fries next to it.

Sid shook his head. "I'm not sure which is more appalling, the amount of food you have there, or its fat content."

"It's good stuff," I said with my mouth full. "Want a fry?"

Sid grimaced and pulled back. "No thank you."

I swallowed. "Your, uh, friend with the teeth."

"Who?"

"You know. When I called you."

"Oh, her."

"She wouldn't happen to have been a Sunland Products employee, would she?"

"Nope." Sid sighed as I shoveled a huge bite of chili, cheese, chopped onion and french fry into my mouth. "They're all gone."

"What?"

"They took off this morning. My, uh, friend this afternoon told me that they felt they didn't feel right about staying, given the murder, an altogether shocking display of sentiment over corporate spirit. Either that or someone decided a lack of sentiment wouldn't score any points for the company's image."

"That's a very cynical way of looking at it." I mused as I sucked down some shake. "Then again, it would also be very convenient if someone wanted a way out of here in a hurry that wouldn't look suspicious."

"Indeed. That thought crossed my mind also, but there's no real way of confirming it for the moment. I did confirm the departure of the Sunland people with the hotel staff. Our next chance to talk with them will be at Della's funeral."

"When's that?"

"Monday, in San Francisco. That's where her parents are."

"You want me to go with you?"

"It could be useful, but I think not. Showing up as her last lover and possible killer will be bad enough. Having another woman with me would be too tacky. You know what people always assume."

"Too well." I paused to swallow. "Have you found anything else out about the murder?"

"Nope. I haven't even seen Lehrer today."

"I knew something was going right." I smiled and looked at him. "Are you alright?"

"Fine. Why do you keep asking me that?"

I shrugged. "Della was quite a loss for you."

"It was the shock. I hadn't seen her in fifteen years, then to stumble onto her, not to mention the rude awakening by Lehrer."

"Yeah, right. There are all those memories, and what you said about... being with her. You can't pretend those don't get to you."

"Well..." Sid squirmed a little. "Yes, she meant a lot. But I got that out of my system Thursday night."

"Hm."

"What's that supposed to mean?"

"I don't buy it. You've been acting a little funny since it happened. Nothing big, just a little off. Like with the cocaine this morning. You looked like you really wanted some."

"I did." Sid shrugged at my gape. "I told you, it's one powerful high."

"I wouldn't know. But you've also been exceptionally active, even for you. I mean two girls yesterday, another this afternoon. Keep this up, and you'll set a record."

"I'm not interested in scorekeeping."

"I know. That's what's bugging me. It's like you're trying to make up for Della or forget her."

Sid studied the floor. "Not so much forget as..." The moment passed. He chuckled. "Either way, you wouldn't believe the offers I'm getting."

"I suppose refusing them never crossed your mind."

"I've refused several. Believe it or not, even I can only do so much. I'm not a bull from Montana."

"Then to what do you attribute your immediate popularity?"

Sid laughed lecherously.

"I mean besides that," I snapped.

"I know. I'm sorry. The more immediate attraction must be the glamor and thrill of living dangerously."

"I don't get it."

"How healthy can sleeping with a murder suspect be?"

"I don't know. Have you picked up any diseases lately?"

Sid laughed. "I've been taking precautions. How about you?"

"Me?"

"It's part of what took me so long to get over here. Marcia called. She said Lehrer has decided you have as good a motive as any, and he's pushing the theory that you killed Della out of jealousy."

"That's ridiculous. He knows we're not sleeping together. What have I got to be jealous of?" I took a huge bite of my burger.

"It's your secret desire to sleep with me and you can't bear that another woman is."

"Make that plural, and it's no secret I'd like to sleep with you. But I'm certainly not jealous. Heck, I'm your friend. That's infinitely better than being a one night stand in my book."

"Not necessarily in everyone else's."

"That's why there are one night stands."

"Fortunately for me."

I wiped my mouth. "Well, at least there's no evidence."

"I doubt that will stop Lehrer from manufacturing some. We'll have to really keep an eye on him and our noses clean."

"To be sure." I stretched then gathered together the wrappings from my lunch. "What are you going to do for the rest of the day?"

He shrugged. "Not much really. With the Sunland people gone and Lehrer on the prowl, I don't know that there's much I can do. Why don't I stick around here, if I'm not in the way."

"Why not?" I looked at the cases all over the stockroom. "You could even help."

"Doing what, pray tell? They're not exactly lining up out there."

I pointed to the wall displays. "See all those rafts and beach towels and all that water ski equipment? They have to be taken down and packed away, then all these boxes here in the stock room opened, checked in, priced and put out, along with the winter displays."

"And do I get paid for this?"

"The same as I'm getting paid." I grinned.

"Let's see, that's contributing to your eventual inheritance, but nothing beyond that. Am I right?"

"You'll also get my undying gratitude."

"Oh, goody. Better than minimum wage." He slid out of his jacket.

"Hey, don't. I was just teasing."

"I may as well."

"Why not go back to the hotel and catch up on some of the sleep you've been missing?"

Sid grinned sheepishly. "Actually, I already did that. I was pretending to be asleep to get rid of Lynn and really did conk out. I didn't wake up until Marcia called at two thirty."

"I mean it, Sid," I said, putting my hand on his arm. "Don't do anything you don't want to do. If you want to hang out here, fine. Just do me a favor and keep your hands off the customers."

"Might be good for business."

"It would ruin my father's professional image."

Sid slid his watch chain into his vest pocket and

opened his vest.

"Alright, I'll be nice and conventional. Where do we start?"

"You really don't have to. I mean, at least it'll come back to me sooner or later."

"Lisa, I don't mind. I'm serious. Maybe I'll do a behind the scenes piece on the retail industry. This counts as research. I should be able to find a way to take it off on my taxes."

"Alright." I looked at the shelf next to the desk and sighed. "We probably should get the shelves cleared and organized first."

Starting next to the desk, we went to work. By six, we'd cleared a good third of the stockroom. I sent Alice on her break, while Sid kept working.

Five minutes later, Fletcher Haddock walked in, just what I didn't need.

"What are you doing here?" he asked, startled. "Where's- I mean, didn't you say you were a secretary?"

"Yeah, I'm just helping out. My dad owns the place, remember?"

"Right. Yeah."

"Can I help you find something?"

Fletcher looked around. "No, actually. I, uh, came in to talk to the manager." He flashed his name badge. "You're one of our customers."

"He's not here."

"No, huh?" Fletcher thought that one over. For a second, he seemed worried, but I couldn't be sure. All of a sudden, he smiled. "Well, that's that. Say, when do you get off?"

"Late." I fidgeted with the register keys.

"I'll bet I can get us into a midnight show tonight."

"No thanks, Fletcher. I figure I'll be pretty tired."

He hesitated. "Look, you've still got my card, right?"

"Yes, I do." I wasn't sure where it was, but I didn't want to give him an excuse to give it to me again.

"You be sure and call me, okay?"

"We'll see. I'm usually pretty busy."

"No hard feelings about Thursday night?"

"No."

"I just want to talk, I swear. Promise you'll call me?"

"Fletcher, I don't even know when I'm going to get home at the rate things are going."

"Anytime you've got problems and want to talk, I'll be there. I'm serious." And strangely enough, he seemed sincere.

"Fine. I'll do that."

"Alright. I'll talk to you later."

I slumped onto the stool. Sid had the decency to wait until Fletcher was gone before coming to the stockroom door.

"Who was he?"

"Fletcher Haddock." I shook my head.

"Someone from your distant past?"

"Not unless you want to count Thursday night. He seemed really nice."

"I take it he wasn't."

I kicked at a spot on the floor. "We had a really nice time. We walked around. He tried to show me how to bet odds at craps. We talked. He's even Catholic. Said he sings in the choir."

"So what happened?"

"He walked me to the room, stuck his tongue down my throat, then tried to con me into letting him in."

"With the intent of having you for a nightcap."

"Where do these guys get the idea that we're going to fall for their lines? I'm so sick of it. I lay it all out, right up front, and they still assume I'll say yes. And the thing that really annoys me is that Fletcher says he goes to church. Why the heck isn't he practicing it? I really hate that half way attitude. It's what gives Catholics a bad name. I mean what's wrong with just dating? Why does every guy I meet think of me as a potential wife or a one night stand? I'm so sick of it. Fletcher says he just wants to talk. If I've got problems, he'll be there. Sure, he will. He's after only one thing, but do you think he'll admit it? No. The jerk is practically howling at the moon, and he thinks I haven't figured out his game plan. It's bad enough I fell for it Thursday night. And of course, just to make things really perfect, I walk into the suite and what do I get? The sounds of passion, live and in concert from your bedroom."

"I'm sorry," said Sid.

It suddenly dawned on me what I'd said.

"Oh, Sid!" I blinked back the tears. "I'm sorry. I shouldn't have been so thoughtless. I shouldn't even be bothering you with this."

"It's not bothering me, Lisa. This guy obviously hurt you."

"Not as badly as you're hurting now."

"I'm not hurt so bad that I can't be there for you." He came over, lifted me from the stool and held me. "Come on. It's your turn to lean on me."

I slid my arms around his waist. "Sid, I..."

"Sh. It's alright." He pressed his lips to my hair.

The door jangled. I scrambled away from Sid just in time to see Lehrer come straight for the counter.

"Well, well, well," he growled. "And what do we have here?"

"Can I help you, Investigator?" I asked coldly.

Lehrer hesitated, looking us over, then nodded. "You two are coming with me down to the station."

Sid sighed. "Just one moment, while I get my jacket."

"Hold it, Sid," I said. "We don't have to go anywhere with him. He's out of his jurisdiction. We're in California, remember?"

Lehrer snorted. "Yeah, well, I need some questions answered, and you two had better cooperate, or I'll get a California warrant."

"So ask," said Sid.

Alice had to come back from her break just then. I sent her behind the counter and moved the rest of us to the stockroom.

Lehrer dug out a notepad and pen. "Alright, Hackbirn, where do you live?"

"In Beverly Hills," said Sid, adding the street address.

"And you, Wycherly?"

I hesitated. "It's the same address."

Lehrer looked me over and smirked.

"We're not lovers!" I snapped.

"Oh really," replied Lehrer. "How long have you two known each other?"

"A little over a year," said Sid.

"You say you write for magazines."

"Yes," said Sid. "As a matter of fact, you can find my column in On Our Own. I believe I saw this month's issue in the gift shop back at the hotel."

"This month's Forbes has that budget piece," I added.

"Really?" Lehrer looked me over again.

"Lisa is my secretary and only my secretary," said Sid with that edge to his voice that means he's getting really angry.

"How long you known Della Riordan?" Lehrer asked.

"It's hard to say," said Sid. "We hadn't seen each other in a lot of years when we met again by chance Thursday night."

"What do you know about how she made her living?"

"I knew she was an accountant."

"Did she say anything about any side businesses?"

"No."

"Didn't ask you to hold anything for her?"

"No. What are you leading up to?" Sid looked Lehrer over carefully.

"Well, a California police department asked to keep an eye out for Ms. Riordan. It seems she was here to make a little drug delivery, and we are cooperating with the Sunnyvale P. D."

I held my breath. Sid shrugged.

"If Della was interested in anything besides catching up on old times, she certainly didn't tell me about it," he said without batting an eye.

"That's good, Hackbirn," said Lehrer, puffing himself up. "That's real good. You just keep watching your step. Things don't look too good for either of you, especially what I saw when I came in."

He sauntered out. I just barely kept my mouth shut until I was sure Lehrer was gone.

"Of all the no-good, lousy..." I screamed in frustration.

Sid smiled softly. "Rats. For a second there, I thought you were actually going to swear."

I kicked the shelf. "Why does he have to be so obnoxious?"

"I think what he said about Della is a lot more interesting." Sid leaned on the desk.

"What do you mean?"

"That little drug delivery?"

"You mean that cocaine was Della's?"

"Must be. It accounts for that pro who went over her room. Della must have spotted a tail and dropped the box in your purse."

"And it was right next to her, too." I sat down in the desk chair. "Oh great. I hope we don't get searched again."

"Don't worry. I put the goods in the false bottom for the moment. What do you want, Alice?"

She leaned in the doorway. "What was that all about?"

"That woman that was murdered the other night," I said.

"Ooo." Alice's face scrunched up in disgust. "Does Lehrer think you guys did it, or something? He's, like, such a jerk." The door jangled. "Gotta go."

"We should probably destroy that box," I said as soon as I heard Alice talking to the customer.

"Possibly. We still have an operative to dispose of. A couple counts of possession wouldn't hurt."

"True." I sighed and looked at my watch. "Sheesh. It's after seven. I thought I was getting hungry."

Sid snickered.

I glared. "We are two hours late for dinner. That's a long time even for you."

"It is at that." He smiled. "I've got an idea. Why don't we get changed? You get a dress on. I'll clean up. Then we'll go get dinner and hit the tables."

I shrugged. "Don't you want to engage in your usual extra-curricular activity?"

"Nope." He rolled down his sleeves and put the cufflinks back in. "To be honest, if you'll pardon the expression, I'm pretty much petered out for the moment."

[It went right past you. You didn't even blink - SEH]

"Oh. Why don't we just play cards in the suite?"

Sid looked me over as he buttoned up his vest. "Why don't you want to go out?"

"Well..." My face felt hot. "It's going to sound really stupid, but it's your reputation. I mean people are already talking, and with Lehrer trying to push me killing Della in a fit of jealous passion..."

Sid nodded. "That is a point. However, I doubt staying in the suite is going to do anything to put those rumors to rest. If anything, an early evening could make it worse."

"Yeah, I guess it would."

Sid put his fingers on my chin. "Lisa, people are going to talk no matter what we do. I say to hell with them. Talk can't do a thing to us, so we've got nothing to lose by it, and like the song says, that's freedom."

"You're right." I got up. "I guess I'm a little worried about my parents finding out, but really, if they can't handle it, it's their problem."

I grabbed my purse and we sauntered out. On the sidewalk, Sid's arm floated down across my shoulders.

"I hope you don't expect me to play high stakes," I said. "I refuse to bet more than I'm prepared to lose."

"I can front you, if you like, for a cut of the proceeds, of course."

"What if I lose?"

"But, my dear, you forget I am one lucky man." He smiled and gave me a quick squeeze. "An incredibly lucky man. So relax. We'll go blow some bucks and have a good time."

We did, too, furtive stares notwithstanding. And gambling with Sid was a blast. He is incredibly lucky and it rubbed off on me for a change. I actually left the casino with three times my original stake.

September 18, 1983

Sid must have fainted when he found I'd gotten up early enough to make it to eight a.m. mass the next morning. [Damned near - SEH] But I was hoping to avoid people I knew at my old church. I still ran into Neff and Mary. Mary tried to make me feel guilty and Neff told me something that had me speeding on the way back to the hotel. (Sid had told me to take the Mercedes the night before.)

I burst into the suite at quarter after nine and went straight into my bedroom.

"There you are," said Sid, following me. "We may have to vacate. I haven't checked with the desk yet, but I only reserved this suite through this morning."

"I'm vacating anyway." I opened my suitcase and threw the clothes I'd left out into it.

"You don't have to yet. Check out's not 'til eleven, and if the hotel doesn't need the room, we can stay."

"You can stay where you like." I hurried into the bathroom to collect my toiletries. "I'm changing."

"What's the matter?" Sid came to the bathroom door.

"My folks are back in town!" I quickly tightened the tops to my shampoo and conditioner before tossing them into the carry-on bag. "They got back last night."

"So?"

"Sid, Daddy can't stand you as it is." I grabbed the carry-on and pushed past Sid into the bedroom. "And you have never seen him really mad. When he catches me in this suite with you, he is going to be really mad."

"We already live in the same house." It's Sid's house really, and our bedrooms are on opposite ends.

"Well..." Flushing, I jammed my nightgown into the suitcase.

"Oh hell. Don't tell me you still haven't told them."

I had kind of forgotten to tell my parents about living with Sid when he hired me.

"I just haven't gotten around to it," I said. "It's not a simple thing to toss at them, especially since it's been a year, and you know Mae won't let me bring it up whenever they're visiting, and I hate doing it over the phone. And of course, Neff and Mary told them all about the trouble here, and they're worried, so if you don't mind, I'm changing rooms, preferably on a different floor, maybe in another hotel, maybe I'll even change states."

I looked around for my deck shoes.

"Oh, come on, Lisa," groaned Sid. "You're overreacting. We're in two separate rooms."

"That's not near far enough for Daddy."

"He's more reasonable than that."

"Not when he's mad. Where are they?"

I looked under the bed. The shoes were there, but beyond them was something else. I grabbed a towel that had fallen near the foot of the bed and covered my hand with it.

"Don't tell me those deck shoes of yours finally started growing something," said Sid. He hates my deck shoes.

"Real cute, Sid." I reached and pulled the handgun out from under the bed. "Why do I get the feeling that someone didn't just forget to pack this?"

Sid shook his head. "I knew I should have wired this place. Whoever visited us last night also dropped a pair of six-inch platform shoes in the coat closet, and while you were at church, I found an extra long pair of black slacks in your suitcase."

"I'm being framed," I whispered.

"It's pretty sloppy except for that gun. What do you want to bet it's the one that killed Della?"

"I don't." I sank onto my bed, feeling a little faint. "But who would want to frame me?"

"Della's killer, or possibly our friendly neighborhood

enemy operative, assuming that's the gun that killed her." He took the gun. "I'm taking this and the other stuff to the sheriff's department this afternoon."

The door buzzed.

"I'll get it," I said mechanically, then went. Sid slid quickly into his room.

I can't say my father looked happy when I opened the door. Tall and broad shouldered, he has that rugged mountain man look about him, right down to the strong silent demeanor. Mama, on the other hand, was bubbling over. She's small, with bright, flashing eyes. They're both from southern Florida and still have fairly strong accents.

"Lisle, baby!" Mama crowed, throwing her arms around me. Lisle is my parents' pet name for me.

"Hi, Mama," I said, still nervous.

I hugged her, then Daddy.

"Hi, honey," he said, then pulled back. "What the hell are you doing here? Why didn't you call us?"

"William Wycherly, you can just stop that right now," said Mama. "Lisa has a right to do as she pleases." She looked at me. "But, honey, I really wish you would have called."

"I did, Mama," I said. "But you guys were out of town, and the assignment came up so fast and we couldn't wait."

"Oh, Sid, there you are." He was coming out of his bedroom. Mama went over and gave him a warm hug. "How are you, honey?"

"Just fine, Althea." Sid smiled back. He and Mama really like each other. "How are you?"

"Real well." She wandered around the sitting room. "Bill, isn't this nice? I been dying to see inside one of these suites for years. Lisle, no wonder you wanted to take advantage of us being gone. Isn't this nice, Bill?"

"Nice enough," grumbled my father. He shot a brief glare at Sid, who mercifully ignored it.

Daddy, unfortunately, is not very tolerant of effeminate males, and he considers Sid's urban polish sissified. He is also convinced that Sid is going to turn me into a fallen woman. But the really weird thing is that Daddy is extremely jealous of Sid.

"Two bedrooms, too," said Mama. "See? I told you, Bill, there wasn't a thing to worry about. It was just people talking. Landsakes, can't trust your own daughter."

"Oh, I trust Lisle." Daddy sent another quick glare Sid's way.

"Well, Sid, how long y'all got this room paid up for?" asked Mama.

"We're fine here, Althea," said Sid.

"Uh-huh." Mama gave him a shrewd once over. "I don't want to hear any arguments. You two just pack yourselves up and head on over to the house. Lisle, put Sid in Mae's old room."

"I don't want to impose," said Sid.

"Landsakes! You're not imposing."

Sid looked over at Daddy.

"Won't take no for an answer," Daddy said, which surprised me. I mean Daddy wouldn't have said no, but I got the feeling he really wanted Sid at the house. [He wanted me where he could keep an eye on me - SEH]

"Honey, I'd never forgive myself if I let y'all stay at this big expensive hotel, eating bad hotel food." Mama smiled and took Daddy's arm. "Now, Bill and I gotta get to mass. We'll meet y'all back at the house."

"Alright, Mama," I sighed. "Oh, wait." I looked at Sid for help, but he had no idea what I wanted. "Um, it might take a bit. We- we've got an errand to run."

Sid shot me a puzzled glance, then played along. But Daddy caught him. Glaring at me, he folded his arms.

"Young lady, what the hell is going on here?"

"Nothing, Daddy." I swallowed nervously.

"Oh, really now. Not when I been hearing all sorts of rumors, even people saying you went and killed somebody."

Mama glared at Daddy. "Now, Bill, you know

that's hogwash."

"I never said it wasn't." Daddy's big, round, angry eyes fixed themselves on me. "But something is going on around here, and, Lisle, you're acting just a hair too guilty not to owe me an explanation."

"Well, I..." Frantic, I looked to Sid for help, which was pretty stupid given how sure Daddy was that Sid was the cause of it all.

Sid took a deep breath. "There's very little to explain, really. It was just an unfortunate coincidence. Thursday night, I ran into an old acquaintance, who I entertained here in the suite. She left to her room and was, sadly, killed there. The sheriff's investigator working the case has proven to be very ill-mannered and has not only accused me of being the killer but Lisa as well. The word has spread, and someone, either a prankster or perhaps even the killer, decided last night to leave some potential evidence in our suite, in order to frame us. And by the way, Lisa, we'd better get on over to the sheriff's department pretty quickly before a search warrant arrives."

Daddy's eyes narrowed. "Which sheriff's investigator?"

"Carl Lehrer," I said.

Daddy swore. "I wouldn't put it past him if he put the stuff in here himself."

"What do you mean, Daddy?"

"Never mind."

"Oh, that Lehrer has had it in for your daddy since he was a motorcycle cop," said Mama. "Remember that deputy who tried to accuse him of taking a bribe?"

"That was Lehrer?" I asked.

"Oh, yes." Mama turned to Sid. "It was about five or six years ago. We found out after it had all happened that Lehrer was short on his ticket quota. He pulled Bill over for an unsafe lane change, only Bill hadn't changed lanes at all. So he took it to court, and of course Judge Davis knew Bill, and he knew Lehrer, and when it looked like Davis was going to find for Bill,

Lehrer got all up in arms and accused Bill of offering him a bribe, which made him look even more ridiculous because everybody knew Bill was the last person to do that, and Lehrer's had it in for Bill ever since. Well, y'all better get to the sheriff's station, and we're late for mass. Come on, Bill."

She took Daddy's arm and steered him out of the room.

"Let's get going ourselves," said Sid, heading into his room.

"What about packing?" I followed him to the door.

He picked up a laundry bag off of his bed. "You can worry about that when we get back. Come on."

I grabbed my purse off the sofa and scrambled after him. The elevator opened just as we arrived, letting off a bellhop and an elderly couple.

"What do you mean I can worry about the packing?" I asked as the doors closed. "You've always preferred doing your own before."

"I'm not packing," he said quietly, then sighed. "I'm sorry, Lisa, but there is no way in hell I am going to stay at your parents' house."

"I knew this was going to happen," I groaned. The elevator opened on the ground floor and we got off. "Sid, can't you please? Just to keep the peace?"

"No." His pace quickened as a sheriff deputy wandered up to the check in desk. We slid around him out to the parking lot and the car.

"Why not?" I asked, getting in.

Sid backed quickly out of the space and took off.

"It has nothing to do with you," he said finally. "But there is no way I can have company at your folks' place."

Doing without was out of the question.

"Do you have to have your own place for that?" I asked.

"Of course not, but I hate presuming on the hospitality of others. The only time it doesn't make things difficult is buying it."

I groaned. "Please, Sid, whatever you do, don't do that. I'll... I'll..."

"Provide services yourself?" Sid asked, with one eyebrow raised and this little smile he has that is about as arousing as a smile can get, and I know he's mentally doing it with me, and I still get goose pimply and hot and bothered over it.

"That's not fair," I grumbled, flushing candy apple red. "It's just that if you buy it, someone will find out, and that much talking, I'm not ready to deal with."

"Lisa, you know I don't unless I'm desperate, and with the offers I've been getting, it's not likely I'll be anywhere near desperate."

"Well, you could rent a room for the evening." I shrugged. "It sounds kind of tacky, but I've heard there are a couple places around that rent by the hour."

Sid laughed. "That's about as tacky as visiting a hooker, and will probably create just as much talk." He shook his head. "I'll just stay in the suite."

"Oh, Sid, please? Mama won't think anything if you just tell her you're visiting someone, and I'll keep Daddy off your back."

"I don't want to stay with your folks."

"For my sake?"

He glanced my way. I blinked twice.

"Alright," he grumbled. [Those beautiful cow eyes of yours strike again. Have I mentioned what a weakness I have for that routine? - SEH] "But we do have a case we're supposed to be investigating, not to mention your friend Murray's disappearance, and remember we do not want your parents to suspect that we're doing anything beyond visiting."

"So that's what we'll tell Mama we're doing," I replied. "She'll believe us, and Daddy will believe the worst no matter what, so if we just stay out of their way, we'll be able to pull it off. There isn't any overt investigating I can do without raising questions as it is."

"True. But that doesn't mean I'm happy about it."

"Neither am I."

Everyone was really nice at the sheriff's station. We turned the gun into Lieutenant Larry Roth, my friend Jimmy's uncle.

"It sure has been a long time, Lisa," he asked going over the stuff. "You like it down there in Los Angeles?"

"Yeah, pretty much."

Uncle Larry picked up the gun and shook his head.

"Where did you find this?" he asked.

"Under my bed at the hotel."

He grinned and shook his head. "I'd almost say Lehrer is up to his old tricks, except this could be the real gun."

"Why do you say that?" asked Sid.

Uncle Larry chuckled. "Lehrer's so lazy he'd make up evidence sooner than work on finding it. Of course, no one can prove he actually has. That's why he's on night shift. He can manage a crime scene okay, but he's not big on routine, just competent enough to keep his job. You can't fire someone for being a jerk. It sure is nice seeing you again, Lisa."

"Nice seeing you, Lieutenant." I paused. "You wouldn't happen to have Jimmy's home phone number, would you? I only ran into him that once, and it wasn't exactly a good time to sit down and chew the fat."

"I'll bet." Chuckling, Uncle Larry scribbled onto a piece of scrap paper. "Here you go, but he's usually sleeping during the day."

"No problem. I've got work. Thanks."

Sid waited until we were back on the road before he asked about Jimmy's number.

"Are you hoping to reignite something?"

"Nothing had ever ignited, to begin with, and he's married now." I shrugged. "You just have your inside source. I have mine."

"Not a bad idea." Sid glanced over at me with a mischievous grin. "But how are you going to coax him into talking?"

I folded my arms and grinned. "If you'd ever turn

that incredible imagination of yours over to something besides carnality, it might occur to you that there are other ways besides physical gratification to gather information."

"You're too cheap to bribe anyone."

"So obvious, Sid. I'm referring to much more subtle tactics."

Sid chuckled. "And I'll bet you'll manage to pull it off one way or another."

By the time we were done packing and paying off the hotel and got out to my parents' house, my parents were already back from mass. As Sid parked the Mercedes in the driveway, Murbles and Richmond came running up, barking their deep roaring barks. They're so huge, they can be pretty intimidating. Sid at least had the sense not to let on if he was. He did hesitate before getting out of the car until he saw me getting out.

"Here, Murbles. Here, Richmond," I called. They came running over and bounced and pranced around me. I cuddled each one. "How are my sweet puppies? Huh? How are my sweet little babies?"

"They are hardly babies," said Sid, shutting the door.

Murbles whined a little as he went over and sniffed at Sid. Sid hesitated then gave Murbles a quick scratch behind the ears. Richmond came over to investigate and got the same perfunctory scratching. I looked at Sid, puzzled.

"You don't seem to dislike dogs," I said.

"I neither like nor dislike them," he replied. "Dogs are dogs. I haven't had that much contact with them, really."

"You poor deprived urbanite." I cuddled my sweeties some more. "I always figured you didn't have any pets because you didn't like animals."

"I have no problem with house pets. It just never occurred to me to acquire any."

"There you are," called Mama, coming out onto

the porch. "Bill! They're here! Bill will help with the luggage, Sid."

Sid opened the trunk. Daddy appeared from around the corner of the house.

"This all yours?" Daddy asked picking up the two suitcases.

"No. That one's Lisa's." Sid pointed.

"Matching luggage." Daddy glared at Sid.

It matched because Sid and I had had to travel as husband and wife on other Quickline business, but I was really going to tell my dad that.

"Daddy," I groaned. "Sid just loaned me one of his because my stuff was so beat up. Just friend to friend, okay?"

Daddy looked at Sid. Sid smiled back, even if it was forced. Daddy went on into the house and we followed.

"Welcome to the Hotel California," muttered Sid, and promptly received one of my elbows in his ribs. He nearly stumbled as Murbles brushed past him onto the porch and to the door. "Are the dogs allowed in?"

"Of course they are, Sid," said Mama, petting Murbles. "They're part of the family. Aren't you, Murbles, baby?" Richmond nosed his way in for his share of the affection. "We've had Murbles since before Lisa got out of high school, and then she brought us Richmond four years ago. Poor little puppy had been abandoned. Lisle, why don't you show Sid around the house, then y'all get settled in and we'll go to lunch."

"It's very kind of you to put me up," said Sid politely.

"Well now, it's my pleasure, sweetheart, and Lord knows, we don't get to see near enough of Lisa. You two take your time settling in, and for heaven sakes, Sid, get out of that suit and into something more comfortable. Landsakes, you look like you're going to a funeral."

"Funeral," Sid groaned. "Bless it all. I've got to go to Della's funeral tomorrow. How long does it take to drive to San Francisco from here?"

"Oh, not even five hours," said Mama.

"Driving speed limit, of course," I said.

"Well, of course, he does, Lisle," said Mama.

Sid shook his head. "I'll confess. I've been known to press my luck and the accelerator a bit." He figured in his head. "Five hours at fifty-five, that would be... Let's see, the funeral's not til eleven. I should be able to make it if I leave by seven."

"Oh, goody. No running," I said.

"'Fraid not," said Sid with an evil grin. "We'll just run at five thirty."

I groaned. Mama laughed.

"Bill and I will be waiting for y'all in the kitchen." She wandered off.

"Well," I said, taking his arm. "Welcome to a bit of my personal history."

We went into the living room first. Sid spotted the piano and went over to it.

"That's from when Mae and I took lessons," I explained. Mae is my older and only sister.

Sid played a major scale. He's been playing since he was six, and he's really good.

"Hm. Still in tune."

"You can play later. I'm sure Mama will insist on it."

"I'm sure she will." Sid smiled and followed me into the dining room. I pointed out the kitchen, then led him back through the entry into the back of the house.

"This is our bathroom over here," I said, pointing to the door at the end of the hall. "And my parents' room is in here."

We poked our heads in.

"One bed," Sid observed dryly. "What a surprise. Of course, that doesn't mean he still does."

"Sid! That is out and out insulting."

"I'm sorry."

"No, you're not. Things aren't going to get any better between you two if you insist on keeping that kind of attitude."

"Things aren't going to get better as long as I'm around you."

"You're not helping, and you might at least make an effort."

"What about him making an effort?"

"I'll talk to him, but it goes two ways, remember."

He sighed. "I'll try. What's next?"

"My room." I led him down the hall. "Mama's changed the curtains and bedspread and repainted, but it's still my old furniture, and some of my old Shakespeare posters are still on the walls. She had them framed."

The phone rang, but I ignored it. Sid nodded, then followed me to Mae's room.

"It's technically the guest room," I said. "Mae's been gone for over ten years, but we still call it her room. There's a trick to the closet door. You have to lift it onto the track like this or it sticks." I demonstrated. "It's been like that since I was eight. Mae caught me pasting ape pictures from National Geographic all over her Tiger Beat Magazine. You know, the one that had all the teen heartthrobs in it? She got so mad she knocked me right into the closet. I got five stitches right here." I pulled up my hair and showed Sid the spot. "And Mae got grounded for a week."

"Didn't you get punished? After all, you were the instigator."

"I had to buy her all new magazines. I was hurt so bad, Daddy said it was punishment enough and I deserved what I got, even if Mae had no right to do it. Daddy's tried time and again to fix the door, but it just won't stay fixed."

Mama came in.

"I hope you two can stay through the end of the week," she said. "That was Mae on the phone just now. Darby and Janey have off Thursday for a teacher in-service day, and Neil decided they might as well skip Friday, too, and come on up for the weekend. They'll stay Wednesday night with Neil's aunt in Sacramento, then be up Thursday."

Neil is Mae's husband. Besides Darby and Janey, they also have Ellen, Marty, and Mitch.

"Will there be room?" Sid asked. The O'Malleys adopted Sid a couple months after I had started working for him, which was a little surprising since Sid is not overwhelmingly fond of children. But Mae's kids adore him and he's very close to them.

"We've got a couple vacant cabins," said Mama. "We'll give one to Mae and Neil, and the kids can camp out in the living room. They always think that's such a treat. I just hope y'all can stay. The kids'll be so thrilled to see you. Of course, I do hope all that trouble is cleared up by then."

"I think we can stick around even if it is," said Sid.

"That's perfect. Now, come on, Lisle. Let the poor man get changed in peace so we can go to lunch."

Sid showed up in record time wearing a shirt, sweater, and tight designer jeans. Mama piled us into the jeep as Daddy gazed thoughtfully at the fenders.

"Althea, didn't you take this to the car wash before we left?" he asked, puzzled.

"I sure did, Bill. What's the matter?"

"There's mud all over the fenders."

I swallowed. "Didn't you drive the jeep to church this morning?"

Daddy shook his head. "Weren't anyplace to get mud on it then."

"It must've happened on the way back from the car wash," said Mama. "That's right. I stopped at Raley's to pick up some Tylenol and it was raining when I got out."

Daddy didn't seem convinced, but let it go.

"There's a new little Mexican place we're going to," said Mama. "It's really nice, and your Daddy loves it 'cause they have those jalapeno peppers and those nasty little serrano things."

"Really?" Sid's interest was definitely piqued. So

was mine. We both love spicy food, the hotter the better.

It had come as a bit of a surprise to us since Sid's system is pretty touchy and while I'll eat almost anything, I don't really come across as someone who would enjoy eating fire. But earlier that July, we found a bag of different chiles on our doorstep. It turned out one of Sid's girlfriends had brought it over as a joke. She plants chiles to keep pests out of her garden, but can't stand the product. She figured Sid would laugh, then throw them away. Sid and I arm wrestled each other for the last serrano.

At the restaurant, the waiter brought us a bowl of raw jalapenos and serranos right away. Daddy helped himself, but Sid hesitated.

"What's up?" I asked him.

"Party tonight," he said quietly.

"Oh." I knew what the problem was. "I've got the Alka Seltzer in my purse. It should be out of your system in time."

Sid took a couple jalapenos while I munched on a serrano. Daddy had already broken a sweat.

"Landsakes, Lisle," said Mama. "The things you got in your purse. Why are you carrying Alka-Seltzer?"

I laughed and swallowed some water. "It's from last week. Sid took me for Indian food. I swear, Daddy, you would have loved it. We were swimming in sweat by the time we were done."

Daddy's eyes narrowed. "Are you two dating?"

"I take Lisa specifically because we are not," said Sid, his voice getting that angry edge to it. "The after effects of such a meal not exactly being conducive to romance."

"You can say that again," I replied laughing. "Between the two of us, it's worse than the campfire scene in Blazing Saddles."

Sid glared at me. Little beads of perspiration had popped out all over his forehead.

"Sorry," I said quickly.

"Lisle, 'tisn't nice," said Mama.

"Well, it's not that big a deal," I said, eating a jalapeno.

Sid chuckled in spite of himself. "It is when I'm stuck in a closed car with you."

"You're no bundle of roses yourself, pal," I replied, wiping my forehead. "At least I give you some warning. Those SBD's of yours are beyond description."

"I've about had enough of this," growled Daddy.

The waiter brought us killer salsa, made with fresh chiles and tequila, and took our orders. I scarfed, Sid ate more than usual, and Daddy glowered.

"Bill, y'all planning on going in to the store tomorrow?" Mama asked as we finished eating.

"Oh, my god," I gasped. "Daddy, we've got a problem."

"What's the matter?" he asked, glancing at Sid.

"It's Murray," I said. "He's disappeared. I went by the store yesterday at eleven and it was closed. I went ahead and opened and called around, but no one knows where he is."

"Any cash missing?"

"No, and the night deposit bag was still there. I checked it, and the deposit balanced with the register tape. Are those gambling rumors true?"

Daddy stifled a belch then nodded. "'Fraid so. He weren't too bad about it, but he did have a problem. I told him the first time any money's missing, he was out the door."

"But the money was all there, and the police said his car was at his apartment. They even broke in, just in case he was hurt or something, but he wasn't there."

Daddy shook his head. "I guess I'll have to go down and take over. He sure picked a lousy time to run off, with winter changeover on the doorstep."

I grinned. "I already started that yesterday. Sid helped. We got a lot done."

"That was real nice of you, Sid," said Mama. "I hope Lisa didn't push you into it."

"He volunteered, Mama," I said quickly. "I even

told him not to."

"Well, that was really sweet," said Mama. "Wasn't that, Bill?"

Daddy reluctantly nodded.

"Listen, Daddy," I said. "Why don't I just keep running things down there while I'm here, or you can find Murray or someone else."

"If you don't mind, Lisle," he replied. "I'd just as soon have you as anyone else."

Sid, on the other hand, would just as soon have had someone else. But he didn't say anything. He quietly pressed the back of his hand to his lips. I got out the Alka Seltzer.

"It's time for the toast," I said, opening the box. "Daddy, you want some?"

Chuckling, Sid placed his water glass in front of me. Daddy hesitated but added his glass. I fished out the ice, then dropped the tablets in. We waited a moment for the tablets to dissolve, then Sid and I each took our glasses and clinked them together.

"Cheers," I said.

"Bottoms up," he said.

"Daddy?" I asked.

He just clinked my glass, and the three of us drank and grimaced.

"Man, this stuff tastes aw-" I didn't get any further because this horrendous belch took over.

"Lisle!" gasped Mama.

Sid sat back and laughed quietly. Daddy laughed loud and hard.

"It was an accident," I groaned, beet red.

"Of course it was, honey," said Daddy, wiping his eyes.

"Let's just be thankful for open cars," said Sid.

We looked at each other and laughed. Daddy's eyes narrowed and he glared at Sid even harder.

Back at the house, Mama coaxed Sid into playing the piano. Daddy disappeared. I started to go after him, but Mama stopped me.

"He just needs to be left alone," she said.

She and Sid spent the afternoon chatting, while I fretted. But there wasn't much I could do. Daddy showed up for dinner and was less than enthused when he found Sid had been helping Mama. He disappeared again right after eating. Sid and I cleaned up while Mama went to talk to him. She came back, shaking her head.

"Well?" I asked.

"He's as stubborn as they come," sighed Mama. "Just pay him no mind, Sid. He's always been this way about anyone who comes near Lisa, and he figures you're closer than most."

"We're just good friends, Althea," said Sid.

"Of course you are, honey." She patted his arm. "That's the best way to be. Lisle, you gonna wear what you got on to that party tonight?"

"What party?" I asked.

"The one you and Sid are going to."

"I'm not going," I said quickly before Sid could. "I'd really rather visit with you and Daddy."

"Now, honey, you got all week."

"Mama, trust me. I'd rather visit."

Mama frowned, puzzled. "I'm happy to have you, sweetheart, but... Sid, are you alright with that?"

"Perfectly alright." He smiled warmly, then checked his watch. "I'd better get going."

"I'll walk you out," I said.

We were silent until we hit the porch.

"You're welcome to come if you want," said Sid, mischief in his eyes as always.

I smiled. "I might except for one thing."

"What?"

"When you say party, it generally translates orgy to the rest of us."

Sid chuckled. "Group sex can be a lot of fun."

"It doesn't sound like it." I grimaced.

"Actually, I'd almost rather be visiting here, myself."

"Even with Daddy around?"

It was Sid's turn to grimace. "He does put a cramp in what would be an otherwise very pleasant evening." He looked at me fondly for a moment. "That's kind of why I'm taking off. Tonight should afford me an opportunity to satiate myself for a while."

"Is that even possible?" I smirked.

"Good question." Sid's hot little smile slipped out. I swallowed. Sid dropped the smile and picked up my hand. "I would like to give your father as little room to carp as possible, if only for your sake."

"Thanks," I said softly.

"But I would like to know why he got so teed off by all those gas jokes at lunch."

"Oh, that." I laughed. "Passing gas is kind of an old family joke. That's why Mama was so uptight. You just don't talk about things like that in front of people who aren't your family. Then there's Daddy's Aunt Aggie. Back in the Twenties, she ran away to New York City and became a Bohemian. That's why Daddy went to New York to college. Anyway, Aunt Aggie was into free love and very earthy, and she always used to say that the best lovers were the ones you could blow a fart around because then you could be totally honest with them and still be friends."

Sid nodded. "There's some truth in that."

"There's a lot of truth in that. Daddy said all you had to do was substitute the word spouse for lover, and Aunt Aggie was right on the mark." I looked at Sid and shrugged. "He gets jealous of you for some reason."

"Why?"

"I haven't the faintest. I mean, it's not like you're going to take me away from him."

"But I could stain his precious little lamb."

I laughed. "You'd like to think. However, even the ones with the purest of motives have caught hell from him. You're not in bad company, Sid, and the last laugh is on him because I don't want to get married."

Sid smiled warmly and squeezed my hand. "Well,

it's time for me to take off. Would you mind doing me a favor while I'm in San Francisco and stay out of Nevada?"

"I wasn't planning on going," I grumbled sourly.

"Lisa, I know you can take care of yourself. But I still worry. It's only because I care about you."

"I know." I smiled softly at him. "I care about you, too. You be careful tonight, and if I don't talk to you tomorrow, you watch out in San Francisco."

"I will." He reached over and kissed my forehead. "I'll meet you at the store, or come here if you're not there."

"Sure."

He left, and I watched while he backed the Mercedes out of the driveway and drove off.

"I'm going to take a walk down to the horse barns, Mama," I called into the house, then took off myself.

Behind the barn, Daddy was stacking bales of hay onto a rack of pallets under a shelter and cursing to himself about that snake.

"Daddy?" I asked, pretty sure which snake he meant.

"Oh, Lisle." Sullenly, he dumped the last bale.

"What are you so upset about?"

"I'm just worried is all." He sighed. "Honey, why are you so thick with that man?"

"We're friends, Daddy. That's all. Close friends, yes, but nothing more."

Daddy snorted. "He can hurt you so bad. You've had enough man trouble in your life."

"I haven't had hardly any," I said, laughing. I went over and hugged him. "I may have lots of men friends, but there's nobody like you and never will be. Okay?"

"Oh, Lisle." Daddy hugged me back. "You just don't understand, honey."

"I love you, Daddy."

"I love you too, honey." He squeezed me, then let go. "Why don't you help me get the tarp over this hay. We might get some rain tonight."

"Sure. Think we can talk Mama into playing Monopoly with us?"

Smiling, Daddy nodded. "That sounds like fun."

And for the moment, all was right with my world. Who cared about spies and jerk investigators and mysterious packages of cocaine? My Daddy loved me and wanted to play Monopoly with me and that was all that mattered.

September 19, 1983

Sid, having gotten back fairly late from his party the night before, got up too late to go running. I was crushed. I managed to get up early enough to see him off, then headed for the store, getting there at eight thirty.

A liver spotted springer spaniel scratched at the back door and whined as I came up.

"Shoo! Go away!" I hissed at him.

He sat there and looked at me with big forlorn brown eyes and whined.

"You don't belong here," I told him as I unlocked the door.

He barked once, then squeezed past me into the stockroom.

"Hey," I yelped. "Get out of here."

I turned on the lights. The dog barked twice more then sniffed around, looking for something.

"Come on, get out," I said. "You don't belong."

The dog barked again, then scratched at the door leading down to a little rough cellar that Murray sometimes used for extra storage.

"Come," I commanded, getting irritated.

To my surprise, the dog trotted over to me and sat at attention at my feet just as the best obedience trained dog would. Almost automatically, I bent down and praised him.

"Good boy." I scratched his neck. "You obviously belong to someone." He wasn't wearing a collar. "So what's your name?" [I never could understand why people talk to animals as if they could answer - SEH]

The dog barked once.

"What am I going to do with you?" [How was he supposed to tell you? - SEH]

He whined softly. He looked full-grown, maybe a little younger. He whined again. I went over to the desk. Rita had left a note asking if the tuna sandwich in the refrigerator was being saved for any reason. I could have eaten it for lunch, but at that moment tuna didn't do anything for me. The dog whined again.

"Why do I get the feeling you're hungry?" I asked.

He barked.

"How does a tuna sandwich grab you?"

He barked again.

"Okay." I went over to the refrigerator and got out the sandwich.

The dog ate it in seconds.

"You eat almost as fast as I do," I said. I went to the back door and opened it. "Okay, outside with you now."

The dog barked and ran outside. I went back to the desk. As I yawned and stretched, my eyes fell on the phone without really seeing it. But then something else came into focus.

It was innocent enough, one of those promo pen doohickeys that salespeople are always giving out in the hopes that you'll push their product. This one, in red plastic, was stuck to the phone and had a round base, about the diameter of a quarter, and a half inch thick. It had a hole through the middle to hold the pen, which was attached to the base with a thin, tightly coiled cord.

Call me paranoid, but the fact that it advertised Sunland Products and that I was sure I hadn't seen it on the phone Saturday gave me pause. I got my bug finder out of my purse. Sure enough, it flashed, and when I checked the dial, it registered the new pen holder. There really wasn't much I could do about it just then, so I left it and went about getting the store opened.

The dog was sitting next to the front door when I unlocked it. He pushed the door open and ran in, trotting comfortably behind the counter and sitting down in a corner near the register, but out of the way.

"Now wait a minute, buster," I said. "You don't belong here."

The dog just barked twice and stayed put.

He was still there at two o'clock when Rita came in.

"Hello, dog-dog," she said, petting him.

"I take it he's a regular," I said.

"He's Murray's dog." Rita put her purse under the counter. "It's the only thing his wife left him. She took the rest of the dogs with her."

"I thought they raised retrievers."

"No. Springers."

"Oh. Well, that explains a lot. What's his name?"

Rita shrugged. "Murray just calls him dog. You know how he can be. Says he'll name the dog when he sends the papers in to the Kennel Club."

"That dog is at least a year old."

"Just about. Murray's been pretty messed up since the divorce."

"Hm." I looked the dog over again. "If he's Murray's, then he hasn't eaten since Friday. I'm going on my break now anyway. I'll get him some food, too." I patted the dog. "You stay put."

The dog barked but didn't follow me.

I came back twenty minutes later with a can of dog food, a twelve-inch roast beef sub, with provolone, guacamole, and the works, a large bag of Cheetos, a quart of milk and a pint of Haagen Daz ice cream - I passed the freezer section while looking for the dog food. I found the can opener in the desk and retrieved an old pan for gold plate that someone had returned years ago.

I leaned out of the stockroom door into the store.

"Hey, dog, come." He trotted over. "It's chow time, you fool."

The dog yipped and bounced, but did not jump up on me, as I opened the can. I dished up and he could barely contain himself, poor little baby. He whined and yipped. I put the plate on the floor next to the desk, then tucked into my own lunch. The dog gobbled contentedly. In between bites, I scratched his head.

"You need a name, you motley old fool, you."

The dog licked his plate clean and looked at me.

"What do you want, you motley fool?" I ruffled his neck fur with both hands. "Are you a motley fool? Hmmm?"

The dog barked. Okay, he would have anyway, probably, but I took it for inspiration.

"Oh, is that what I'm supposed to call you? Are you the Fool's Motley? How about if we call you Motley for short? You like Motley?"

What he liked was the attention, I guess, and I know he had designs on my Cheetos. So call me a sucker. I gave him a few.

As I finished, I noticed the bug on the phone. Inspiration was in the air. I went to the stockroom door.

"Rita, could you come here for a second?" I asked.

"What's up?" she asked.

"This pen," I said pointing it out. "I didn't see it Saturday. Were the Sunland reps in yesterday?"

Rita shook her head. "I don't think any of the sales reps came in. We were pretty busy yesterday."

"Yeah, I noticed." I'd balanced the register tape from the day before. "Did you stick this here?"

"No." Rita snorted. "One of the reps must have come in and did it while I was helping customers. They are so nervy anymore."

"I'll say. Well, they're not getting away with it this time." I yanked and pulled the bug off the phone and slammed it onto the desk. "The gall of some people."

"I agree."

The bell jangled out front and Rita went to help the customer. I checked my bug finder. No flash. I'd killed it. I picked it up and looked it over. The microphone was in the base. It looked vaguely familiar. I decided to let Sid check it out.

He showed up a little before six. I was taking a

break and playing tug of war with Motley over an old rag. Sid came in from the front.

"Oh hi," I said when I finally noticed him standing in the doorway.

"Hello." He looked at the dog with a puzzled frown. "Would you kindly satisfy my curiosity? A- Why is there a dog in a place of business? And B- Why are you playing with him?"

"He's a total sweetheart," I said. "Apparently, he's Murray's dog and has been abandoned. Rita said he doesn't have a name, so I named him the Fool's Motley, only I call him Motley for short."

"Lovely. Have you considered your position legally with regards to Murray's property?"

"He's a dog, Sid. And besides, somebody has to take care of him until we find Murray."

"I suppose. How was your day?"

I went to the desk. "Largely uneventful, except for my new buddy and this."

I tossed the pen and holder at him. He caught it gracefully and looked it over.

"Uh-oh. Was this here Saturday?"

"Nope. Rita figures some sales rep stuck it on the phone when she was helping somebody yesterday."

Sid examined it more closely. "Curiouser and curiouser. This is a Company bug."

"You think Tom Collins planted it?"

"I think we should ask him, but I doubt it. Remember our target is supposed to have gotten some of their stuff."

"We only have Tom Collins' word on that. What if he went bad?"

Sid shook his head. "I called Henry while I was in the city. He says we can trust Collins. I picked up some other interesting tidbits, too. The DEA is very interested in Sunland Products."

"DEA?" I frowned. "And CIA. How many other acronyms are we going to pull in on this?"

"Well, we're sort of FBI, and there's the IRS.

They're always looking for their cut. But the really interesting part is that Della had called the DEA in."

"What?"

"According to Henry's friend over there, Della was asked to take a delivery to a client in the area. She was told it was just a back order but checked, and it was the coke. She called the police, and the officer she talked to arranged for her to connect with the DEA person here and told her to keep the lid on what she'd found. By the way, the DEA person is undercover and wants to stay that way, too."

"Oh, goody. But why would Della drop the coke on me?"

"She must have panicked. Either she missed her connection or thought she was being tailed. I don't suppose we'll ever know."

I plopped down in the desk chair. "Hm. How was the funeral?"

"Depressing. It was a funeral." Sid leaned against the shelf. "Interesting tidbit number two, though, I picked up a tail at the cemetery. Unfortunately, I had to ditch it."

I grimaced. Ditching a tail usually points up the ditcher as a professional.

"Maybe we'll get lucky and it was the cops," I said.

"It may have been. And speaking of the cops, tidbit number three, I talked to the Sunnyvale police to confirm what Henry told me and found out that they haven't talked to anyone up here about anything, let alone deliveries."

"But what about the guy that talked to Della?"

"He says he only talked to the DEA, and I talked to him as Ed Donaldson, FBI. He had no reason to lie to me."

I shook my head. "Sid, when we're working here as ourselves, wasn't that taking a chance?"

"It might have been, but Henry pointed out that Detective Daly wouldn't have any information on the murder, since he turned Della over to the DEA, and he was right."

"But if it was a cop tailing you."

"Probably someone from up here. Sunnyvale P.D. has nothing to do with this. Of course, it could also have been whoever the cocaine was intended for. Since Della missed her connection, there's got to be some pretty antsy people around here wanting their fix."

I thought it over. "Sid, why would Lehrer tell us Sunnyvale wanted to know about the package when they didn't unless he was looking for it himself and needed an excuse for knowing about it?"

"I've been pondering that myself, as well as tidbit number four, which is that the CIA has got their eye on him."

"Then why didn't Tom Collins say anything?"

"I plan to ask him that very question, but it's always possible he doesn't know. Company people are notorious for not sharing information, and they have their eyes on a lot of people that have nothing to do with secrets."

"But how did Lehrer know about the cocaine in the first place?"

"The obvious answer is that the DEA has stuck their noses in and asked about it."

I looked down at Motley and petted him. "Yeah, that makes sense. He wouldn't say anything about that to us, and he's probably trying to recover it before the DEA does and make himself look good. He sure is working pretty hard to pin Della on me. Of course, that's probably his feud with Daddy."

Sid sighed. "And his animosity towards you seems to have spread to me."

"Well, it's about time I got a little of my own back," I chuckled.

"What's that supposed to mean?"

I got up. "Your reputation has sullied mine beyond repair. I am now a fallen woman, and I haven't even had the fun to deserve it."

Sid's sexy little smile spread across his lips. "I

could take care of that."

I looked out at the front, trying to get my heart to stop its racing.

"Except that I don't care to be a fallen woman in fact," I said turning slowly. "The talk is bad enough, but I do have to live with myself."

"Which is essentially why I'm not doing anything about it." He straightened. "Are you going to stay here all night?"

"No, but I do think I will give Jimmy Roth a call. Maybe I can get some more information on Lehrer. In the meantime, we'd better get home. Mama said she'd hold dinner for us."

"Okay. The car's out front."

I got my purse. "And I've got the jeep. I'll see you over there. Motley, heel."

"You're taking him with you?" Sid was less than enthused.

"Yeah. Rita can't, and somebody's got to take care of him until we find Murray."

"The likelihood of finding Murray is lessening every day. That is going to make things rather sticky legally."

I shrugged. "I'll call your lawyer."

Sid frowned. "I'm not entirely sure I want a dog around."

"But, Sid, we can't just leave him at the pound. They'll kill him. And besides, he's really well trained. He fetches and even finds things I've dropped."

"I'm impressed." Sid sighed. "You'd better be careful about getting too attached to him. He is Murray's dog and Murray could still be alive."

"I hope so."

"Not half as much as I do at the moment."

Motley barked once and looked up at Sid, big eyes shining and tail thumping.

I'd called Mama about Motley, so she was expecting him. Richmond and Murbles weren't too thrilled about a new dog on their turf, but they let Motley alone.

Motley stuck close to me, which didn't make Sid any too happy. He could see what was coming.

I called Jimmy right after supper. It was his night off and he told me to come right over. I took the jeep. Sid decided to join me, only he didn't go to Jimmy's. He had me drop him off at the hotel where we'd been staying.

"I'll take a cab home," he said. "It might be late. I've got a meeting to arrange."

"Okay. I'll leave the door unlocked for you again."

Sid snickered. "Don't bother."

"I wouldn't except Mama and Daddy would wonder how you got in."

"True. Have a nice time."

I pulled away and headed to Jimmy's cabin in the hills above Stateline. It was a tiny three room affair, not counting the bathroom, which was little more than a closet as it was. Terri was a teacher at the local elementary school and had papers to grade.

"I should have done it over the weekend," she said, laughing. "But I got lazy. I'll just work in the kitchen. You two won't bother me at all."

At first, Jimmy and I just chatted about people we both knew, catching up. Most of the kids I'd known in high school either had gotten married or still lived in the area or both. Jimmy knew all about the people who'd stuck around. The only person I'd really kept contact with was Leslie Bowan, and that was sporadic, even if we were still pretty close.

"She's been awfully busy since she got on with that radio station in Denver," I said. "She's already been promoted to news director, and it's an all-news station."

"Did she give up on her anchorwoman dream?" Jimmy asked.

I laughed. "Are you kidding? She's talking a lot to the television people in her area. There just aren't that many tv stations in that market. She wants to go to L.A. and get on a news radio station there, then weasel her way onto one of the independent tv stations and work up from there. She says her biggest handicap is that she's not blonde or a minority."

"That sounds like her." Jimmy sighed. "At least she hasn't changed."

"Oh, she has."

"Maybe. I don't know, Lisa. It seems like everybody's changed, and not a lot of it's for the better. Remember Mike Tipton? He's gone gay."

"He always was," I said sourly. "And that's not necessarily a bad thing."

"And John Leland. He graduated from medical school last May. He got his residency at UCLA. He was at his folks' place all last June. He came over a couple times, but all he could talk about was med school."

I laughed. "And you're saying he's changed? Good lord, John never talked about anything but what he was immediately involved in."

"And what about you?" Jimmy looked at me, his face with a funny pained look.

"What about me?"

"First you turn up in that hotel room with a guy who's sleeping with anything female within reach."

"We're not lovers," I said crossly. "I just work for him."

"I believe you. If you were lovers he wouldn't be running around like that, and I don't think even you would put up with it. It's just you were always so religious."

"I still am," I said. "Sid has different values is all. I respect that and he respects mine. I'd like to think I've always been that way."

Jimmy thought that over. "Yeah. You have. You always made friends with the weirdest people. But you were such a mouse. I mean in a nice way. And the way you told Lehrer off. Lisa, I would have never thought you could be that tough."

I shrugged. "He got me mad. It's Lehrer's problem, as far as I'm concerned. I just can't figure out why he was such a jerk."

"Well, he doesn't like your dad too much."

"He was acting like a total jerk before he knew who I was."

Jimmy shrugged. "That's Lehrer. I hate to say it, but sometimes I think he gets his kicks pushing everybody's buttons. He's always getting yelled at for doing things he's not supposed to, like crossing the state line while he's on duty."

"Why would he do that?"

"You didn't know? Lehrer and Murray Waters are buddy-buddy. Lehrer's always going over to see Murray, usually right around midnight."

"Really? That's weird. I mean what would they have in common?"

"Who knows? I sometimes get the feeling Murray doesn't like Lehrer all that much, to hear him talk."

I feigned interest in my fingernail. "You know Murray?"

"Well, to say hi and stuff. He and my older brother used to hang out until Steve got into Gambler's Anonymous. Did you know Steve?"

"Not well. You do know Murray is missing, don't you?"

"Yeah. I heard about it at roll call Saturday night. Tahoe P.D. asked us to keep an eye out, even though they couldn't do anything officially. We didn't figure it was any big deal because Lehrer said he knew where Murray was."

"He did?"

"Well, something like he knew where to find Murray."

"That's really strange. Has Lehrer found him?"

"Beats me. Sunday and Monday, I'm off."

"It must really stink working nights when your wife's on days. What hours do you work?"

"Eleven to eight. I usually sleep when Terri's at work and get up when she gets home. Days off are a little rough. I have to stay on my work schedule cause it's just too hard to adjust for two days. I'm getting a lot of reading done. If I decide to go to law school, I'll be ready for the LCAT."

"You're going to law school?"

"If and when I get the money."

"Oh, I hope you do soon."

Jimmy looked me over. "Weren't you supposed to go to graduate school? I thought your mom said something about that a couple years ago."

I shook my head. "I got my masters three years ago. I overloaded on credits and did my B.A. in three years and got the master's in one."

"How long have you been working for your boss?"

"Only a year. I was teaching before that. How long have you been with the Sheriff's Department?"

"Since I got out of college. My uncle got me on."

"Yeah, I saw him again yesterday." I blushed. "Turning in evidence."

Jimmy grimaced. "That was pretty weird. Uncle Larry called me right before you did. He was thinking maybe Lehrer planted the stuff until he got the report on the gun. It was the one that killed Riordan."

"Are you serious?" I swallowed. "What is he thinking about it?"

"He's thinking it's too darned bad Lehrer didn't plant it. He's been wanting to bust Lehrer for years." Jimmy noticed me biting my lip and laughed. "He also figures whoever killed Riordan planted it on you. He knows you didn't do it and your boss isn't tall enough to be the guy the waiter saw."

"But the platform shoes."

"They were ladies size six, and who could run in those suckers anyway?"

"Not I." I shook my head. "That's just too weird."

I spent another half hour pumping Jimmy about Della and not answering questions about myself. Jimmy didn't seem to know anything else. Terri looked like she wanted to go to bed, so I left.

I got home around eleven. The door was locked and

I heard piano music coming from the living room. I slid in silently. Sure enough, Sid was at the keys playing one of Chopin's twenty-four preludes, a sure sign that he was bugged.

I sat down on the couch and waited until he had worked his way through the last prelude. He looked over at me.

"I'm taking requests," he said, gazing back at the keys. "However, since your folks are in bed, I'd recommend something soft."

"What's that Beethoven sonata you like? Pata..."

"Pathetique?" He started the first, sonorous chords.

"No, the middle part, the melody." I sang it.

"Ah, the adagio." He played the second movement.

A soft smile crept onto his lips as he concentrated. Whatever was bothering him before, he found some resolution in the dignified, rolling melody.

"Something got your goat tonight," I said softly about halfway through.

He stopped playing. "Tom Collins said the bug wasn't his, but that it's definitely Company equipment."

"In other words, it's the stolen equipment."

"It looks that way. Collins said he's being transferred to a new division. In the meantime, he'll stay on as bartender. Did you find anything out from your friend?"

I nodded and told him what Jimmy had said. He sighed.

"It just doesn't add up," he said.

"We don't have that much information," I pointed out. "We've probably got a few pieces missing yet."

"To be sure."

"When did you get here?"

"A little while ago."

I looked him over. "Did you skip... I mean, I would have thought you'd take advantage of being out."

"I did." His fingers absently went up and down a scale a couple times.

"Did you have a run-in with Daddy?"

"No. We said a few polite words and basically ignored each other. I played a couple numbers for your mother and they went to bed. I kept playing and you came home." He got up. "We'll go running at the usual time tomorrow."

"I can't wait."

He paused for a moment, then went on to his bedroom. I went to mine, wondering what the heck he was so bugged about. [It wasn't the case. It was the woman, and I use the term loosely, that I took advantage of being out with. I believe you knew her in high school as Charlene Dempsey, the cheerleader with the hatchet face, and still as loose as she was then. Probably just as threatened as she was, too. Anyway, when she finally figured out I was the one who knew you, which took a while, she turned pretty bitchy. She made like she thought it was funny, but it really teed me off, enough that when we were cleaning up, I told her so and what I thought of her attitude, which ultimately unnerved me a great deal. I was not just standing up for a friend, but somebody I cared about far more than I wanted to admit at that time – SEH]

September 20, 1983

Sid came with me to the store that morning. He didn't say so, but I got the feeling that he didn't want to be around my father any more than he had to, and certainly not at all without me around. Motley came too.

Sid came dressed to work in a light blue chambray work shirt and his tight jeans. Mama and I had both told him not to worry about it, but he insisted. A big shipment had come in on Monday and I hadn't gotten that much done on the stockroom shelves.

As I unlocked the back door, Motley squeezed past me and went straight to the rough cellar door. I turned on the lights as he whined and scratched at it.

"What's that all about?" Sid asked.

"Beats me." I dropped my purse on the desk and dug out the bug finder. "He did that several times yesterday, too."

"What's behind the door?" Sid walked over to the door.

"Desperation storage. It's basically just a hole in the ground lined with boards." I turned the bug finder on. Nothing.

"Phew!" Sid wrinkled his nose. "Smells like something died down there."

"Probably a rat. It's happened before." I aimed the bug finder into the main store. Still nothing. "We're clean." I looked around the room. "We got the summer stuff down yesterday. Why don't you unpack those boxes from yesterday and pack the summer stuff in there? Wait. We've got to check it against the packing slip and then the order."

Sid pulled a plastic envelope off of one of the cases.

"Let me guess. You unpack something, find it on

here and check it off.”

I grinned. “After counting to make sure you have as many as you’re supposed to unless there’s a back order, which should be noted on the packing slip.” I checked my watch. “I’d better get the money in the register and go open. I can do the balance up front.”

Sid went to work. At ten thirty, UPS came and delivered six more large cases. Sid shook his head.

“Where are you going to put all this stuff?” he asked as the brown van drove off.

“Why don’t you put the summer stuff in the cellar when you’re done packing it? That will get it out of the way at least until we can get the rest of this squared away.”

Sid folded his arms and grinned. “Why do I get the feeling you’re trying to get me to take care of that rat?”

I shrugged. “Just because I don’t like corpses.”

I went out front and Sid went back to work.

Shortly before noon, Alice Martin wandered in.

“How’s it going?” she asked, smiling and leaning on the counter.

“Fine.” I smiled back. “What are you doing here today?”

“Just thought I’d say hi.”

“Don’t you have school?”

“I got a lunch pass.”

“Oh.”

It puzzled me that Alice would suddenly be so friendly. But I didn’t get much time to think about it. Sid came in from the stockroom.

“You’d better call the police,” he said grimly.

“Why?” I asked.

“There is something dead in your cellar, but it’s not a rat. Personally, I’m betting it’s Murray.”

“Oh my god,” I gasped.

“What?” screeched Alice. “Are you sure?”

Sid shook his head. “I have no way of knowing.” Which wasn’t the truth, as I found out a minute later. “I’ve never seen the man. Lisa, maybe you-”

"No," I snapped. "I'm sorry, Sid, but please don't make me. I can't."

Alice bolted for the stockroom.

"It's just a dead body," said Sid, ignoring her. "It can't do anything to you."

"I know." I swallowed. "You can't handle plumbing. I can't handle stiffs. We all have our little weaknesses."

"Alright." He lowered his voice. "He looks like he's been dead long enough to have been killed Friday, which was the last time anyone saw him, I believe."

"Any hints as to what killed him?"

"A nice bloody soft spot on the side of his head."

"Oh, great." I crossed myself as I sank onto the stool behind the register.

"And unless somebody switched wallets, that's Murray down there."

I gagged. "You searched him?"

"It wasn't fun, but yes. We can't count on getting stuff from the police and every little bit helps."

"You're right." I picked up the phone and dialed. "You were lying for Alice about not recognizing him, weren't you?"

"In a manner of speaking. We can't afford to look too competent."

Alice cursed loudly from the stockroom.

"I'd better check on her," said Sid.

They came out as I was hanging up the phone. I picked it up again and dialed the front desk at my parents' place. Alice looked a little pale and a little excited.

"It's him," she whispered. She was obviously shook but also looking forward to telling her friends all about it.

Mary answered at the desk and complained that Daddy was somewhere about the place, and couldn't I call back, and what kind of emergency was it, and oh alright, she'd try to find him. It took less than a minute.

"Hello?" asked Daddy's gravelly voice.

"Daddy, it's me. You'd better come down to the

store right away." I paused. "We've found Murray."

"That's good. Where's he been?"

"In the rough cellar. He's dead, Daddy."

There was a long pause. "I'll be right down."

The police and the ambulance arrived a minute or two later. Sid took them back. I had to stay up front. The detectives were very interested to find Sid involved but upon questioning him, decided that it was a coincidence. They were very nice about the whole thing really.

The morgue wagon showed up, then Daddy drove up just as the lab truck did. I was being questioned about how I found the store Saturday. Detective Simons was none too pleased when he found out Sid and I had rearranged everything.

"We had no way of knowing," I said. "Everything looked like it normally does, except that one shelf was messed up. But there was nothing strange about it."

"Alright." Simons sighed and nodded at the woman from the lab. "We'll have to get prints from you and your friend and anyone else who has a legitimate reason to be here." He looked up. "Afternoon, Mr. Wycherly. You down here for any particular reason?"

"Same reason as you, I expect," Daddy said. He wrinkled his nose. "It sure smells in here."

"We've got the doors open, Daddy," I said.

"Get on one of them down vests, Lisle. It's pretty chilly in here."

"All clear out there?" called someone from the back. "We're bringing him through the front."

"Why?" Simons called back.

"We can't get the gurney around the shelves back here."

I just saw the edge of it, gasped and, trembling, turned my back. Daddy came up and hugged me.

"Honey, y'all can't see anything. He's in a bag."

"I don't care," I sniffed. "It's just too... weird."

Daddy held me close and patted my back.

"Mr. Wycherly, can I ask you a few questions?"

asked Simons.

Daddy looked at me. "They got him in the wagon. You gonna be okay?"

I nodded.

Daddy went with Simons over to the other side of the register. I could see another detective questioning Alice next to the front door. She still looked excited and pleased by the attention, but I also got the feeling she didn't like talking to the police. Passersby on the street stopped and stared. I'd closed the store as soon as the police had arrived, so no one came in. Sid slipped up to my side.

"What's going on in the back?" I asked.

"The usual. Photos, dusting for prints." He shook his head. "I hope they don't send ours in."

"Why?"

"Funny messages pop up when they do, and it will completely blow your cover as a nice local girl gone to work for the writer in the city."

I swallowed. "They want to take ours."

"Then we'd better hope they find prints that don't belong, or it's going to be pretty interesting." His eyes landed on Alice. "I don't know about her. I could have sworn I saw her searching Murray's body."

"Really?"

Sid shrugged. "It's possible she wasn't."

"Today's her day off, too. But she was pretty surprised when Murray turned up."

"And I don't think she faked it either."

"Oh, my god. I've got to call Rita." I picked up the phone and pulled it around the stockroom door to the phone list.

She answered in two rings.

"It's Lisa, Rita. This is really weird. Murry turned up dead in the rough cellar."

"Oh, the poor thing."

"Yeah, well, the police are here now and it looks like they'll be here for a while. Anyway, they said something about taking everybody's fingerprints, so you may as well come on down. I don't know if we'll be open tonight."

"I hope not." Rita paused. "I'll go ahead and leave now. Poor Murray. Do they know how he died yet?"

"I haven't the faintest," I lied. The last thing we needed was to hint to anyone that we might have some experience dealing with stiffs.

"Well, see you in a few."

We all got fingerprinted shortly after I hung up, and then it was mostly just waiting around. Alice tried to stay.

"I can help put things away in the stockroom," she said.

"The police aren't going to want us messing around in there," growled Daddy. "Now, you get on back to school."

"Yes, Mr. Wycherly." Downcast, Alice left.

Rita watched her go. "She sure has been hanging around a lot. She came in last night, too. Said she wanted to know if we'd heard from Murray."

"Hm." My eyes met Sid's briefly.

"I guess I'll be taking off myself." Rita adjusted her purse on her shoulder.

"Thanks for coming down, Rita," said Daddy.

"Anytime, Bill." Rita left quickly.

Sullen, Daddy stepped into the stockroom and looked around.

"Did you get those shelves straight, Lisle?"

"Sid did, Daddy. He's been working really hard and got a lot done. We're almost ahead of things back there."

Daddy looked at Sid, then ambled to the front door.

"Sid did, Daddy." Sid mimicked me in a sour voice. "Will you please quit trying to sell him on me? If the man doesn't like me, there's not much I can do."

"But, Sid-"

"Never mind."

My stomach growled loudly.

"Is that you?" asked Sid.

I checked my watch. "Yeah. It's way past lunchtime."

Motley whined from his corner by the register, where he'd stayed the whole time. I went over and cuddled him.

"Oh, you poor baby," I crooned. "Your master's dead. What are we going to do about you?"

"I probably shouldn't," sighed Sid. "But I'll call Whiteman about him."

Whiteman is Sid's lawyer.

"You will?" I asked, smiling happily.

"I'm not saying we're keeping him. I merely want to know our legal position, just in case."

Daddy came up. "I'm going to see about getting some lunch from the deli. What y'all want?"

I got a cold cut sub. Sid opted for a six-inch turkey sub. While Daddy was gone, Sid called Whiteman. The lawyer said that since dogs are considered property who had rights to the dog all depended on whether or not Murray had left a will. In the meantime, we should inform the police that we had the dog and would continue caring for it until a decision could be made. I looked at Sid. We didn't say anything, but we both had a strong feeling Motley would soon be residing with us.

A twelve-case shipment arrived from Sunland Products around two. The police worked around it. Motley sniffed at each of the boxes. I chuckled and nudged Sid.

"I know," replied Sid. "He did that this morning to the UPS stuff."

"He did that to the other cases, too."

Motley scratched at a box and whined. Sid and I looked at each other. I called Motley off.

"He knew Murray was down in that cellar," I muttered.

"I know. But we can't do anything with all these cops around."

So we waited. The police finally took off just after three. Daddy said he'd take off, too.

"We'll try and get some of this straightened up," I said.

"I'll tell your Mama you'll be home by six," said Daddy. He left.

Sid already had the box knife out and ripped into the box Motley had scratched. It was filled with smaller boxes of trail food. Daddy stocks it year round for the snow packers, and he's about the only one that does. Not that many people like to hike and camp out in eight feet of snow, but we get a lot of summer business from the ones that do and they bring their friends.

As Sid unpacked the boxes, he laid them out. Motley sniffed each one, then scratched at one that looked remarkably like the one Della had dropped in my purse. Sid opened it while I praised Motley.

"Well, what do you know," said Sid, pulling out the plastic-wrapped white powder. "Old Motley here's a coke sniffer."

"Are you sure?"

Sid shrugged. "Well, I'll have to run it through my kit, but I'd give good odds. It would appear there's snow in Tahoe all year round."

"Great. Now, what do we do?"

"Good question." Sid tucked the plastic bag back into its box. "This could be a good motive for Murray's murder."

I grimaced. "It just doesn't make sense. I've known him for years. The gambling I understood, but dealing coke?"

"His dog found the stuff and was obviously trained to do it. Who else in this store had more control over the stock?"

I sighed. "It's from Sunland, too."

"Wait a minute." Sid got up from the floor and paced. "Maybe Della didn't miss her connection, or rather she thought she'd made it."

"What are you saying?"

"She connected you to this store almost immediately. And now that I think about it, she said she was surprised that I wasn't doing drugs."

"In other words, she dropped her package on me thinking I was the person she was to deliver it to." I flopped into the desk chair. "So Murray must have been the connection. But why is he dead, too? And what does any of this have to do with stolen secrets?"

"Both excellent questions, my dear." Sid thought. "However, the answers are beyond reach for the moment. We'd better get as much of this stuff put away as we can so your father doesn't wonder why so little got done and jump to the wrong conclusion."

I rolled my eyes. "Daddy knows I'm not going to do that."

"Perhaps." Sid looked me over with that hot little smile of his. "On the other hand, if there's one thing your father and I have in common, it's an acute awareness of just how much I want to make love to you."

I looked away, flushing. "And he knows how much I don't want to."

"And how very much you do."

He just being honest. But the words caught me funny. I was already getting hot and bothered as it was, and then to have to face it. I shoved through the cases looking for the packing slip.

"Lisa-"

"Sid, don't." I turned and looked at him with a weak smile. "We both know if I tried to compromise myself it wouldn't work. There are times when I think I'm really being an uptight prude, and yet I know I have to accept you the way you are, and I do. It's just that if we were sleeping together, it'd be awfully hard to accept your running around."

"I wish I could understand that. It really wouldn't mean anything."

"Then why do it?"

"It's a basic human need."

"I seem to be doing fine without it."

He smiled softly. "And I don't understand that either. We'd better get to work."

We made it home in plenty of time for dinner. Daddy was a little late.

"I was talking with Les Stevens," he announced, sitting down.

"Oh, is that Darlene's young man?" Mama asked happily. "Darlene is our new cook's assistant, Sid. Her young man just graduated from Davis and wants to come live here in Tahoe to be near her, but hasn't found a job yet."

Sid nodded.

"So he's going to take Murray's place?" I asked.

"Yes." Daddy smiled at me. "Unless you want to take the store yourself, Lisle."

"Now, Bill, you shouldn't joke like that," said Mama with a quick smile although she knew as well as Sid and I did that Daddy wasn't joking. "You know Lisle's very happy working for Sid. Aren't you, Lisle?"

"It's great," I said. "Sid's a terrific guy to work for."

Sid sent me a totally disgusted glance.

After dinner and clean up, I went out to the back porch where my father was on the wide steps. He looked briefly at me, then out again at the cabins and the starlit woods.

"Did the wimp take off again?" he asked.

"Daddy, do you have to?" I groaned.

"You're not so old I'm gonna take back talk from you, young lady."

"Sorry." I plopped down next to him. "Sid went out."

He hadn't planned to, but apparently, our little discussion in the store about our mutual desires got him a little pent up.

"Where'd he go?"

"Beats me. I didn't ask."

There was a pause.

"When's he coming back?"

"I don't know. Probably late. I'll wait up for him and lock up."

Daddy snorted.

I took a deep breath. "Daddy, can I be honest with you?"

"Aw, Lisle, you know you can."

"You haven't been very nice to Sid." I watched as he picked up a twig and shredded it. "I know you haven't said anything to his face, but you do insinuate a lot, and you glare at him all the time. You're really not being very fair to him."

"Honey, you don't understand."

"I understand a lot, Daddy. Okay, his values are different than ours. You don't have to agree with them or condone them. But you could try to come to some sort of an understanding with him."

Daddy glared at his twig shreds. "What do you want me to do?"

"Talk. Just sit down and try to talk out your differences and be honest. I'm not saying you two should be buddies. I just hate all the tension when you two get together."

Daddy tossed the shreds into the night. "If that's what you want, I'll see what I can do."

"Thanks, Daddy." I squeezed him and kissed his cheek. "I love you."

"I love you, too, Lisle." His squeeze was strong but warm. I enjoyed its comfort, then got up and went into the living room to read on the sofa.

My eyes were getting heavy when Mama and Daddy went to bed around eleven. I fought it and continued reading. Or tried to. The words had blurred on the page and my eyes had shut when I heard a soft, familiar, masculine voice in my ear.

"Lisa."

"Mmm." My eyes wouldn't open.

"Time to go to bed."

"Why don't you go, Sid. I gotta lock up." I snuggled deeper into the sofa.

"I already did."

"Dogs inside?"

"Richmond and Murbles are in your parents' room.

Motley is here, ready to follow you.”

“Door locked and bolted?”

“Yes.”

“Good.” I rolled over, facing the sofa back.

He chuckled softly and I felt myself being lifted. I snuggled close against the smooth silk broadcloth of his shirt and the firm chest underneath. Half a minute later, he laid me down on my bed, removed my shoes, and pulled my blankets over me.

“Goodnight, Lisa.”

“Night, Sid.”

His soft lips gently, briefly caressed my forehead.

September 21, 1983

The morning was cold. Sid and I wore down vests over our warm-ups suits as we ran. Motley trotted along next to us as he had the day before, keeping pace perfectly. Little clouds of fogged breath followed us all the way.

It was a good thing Sid showered first. I was so chilled, I stayed in the shower until the hot water ran out, and was late to breakfast.

Daddy took off as I came in, but only because he had to show Les Stevens how to run the store.

"You want me to help?" I asked.

"Naw," said Daddy. "Why don't you stay here and visit."

"Okay."

Mama shook her head as Daddy left. "He sure picked a fine time to leave you here. It's my morning to help at the library. I'd cancel it, but the school kids are coming in and Patty's short-handed as it is."

I shrugged. "I haven't been riding since I got up here."

"Well, what about Sid?"

"I've got some notes to organize and some calls to make," he said smiling.

"There you go." Mama gave me a meaningful glance. "I'd better get going myself. Can you clean up, Lisle?"

"Sure, Mama." I sulked as she gathered her purse and left.

Sid looked at me, puzzled. "I'll help you clean up."

"You don't have to." I finished the last of the toast and got up.

"It's the least I can do." Sid gathered plates.

"Sid, you're a guest. You're supposed to let us do

it."

"Aren't you a guest, too?"

I sighed. "I'm family." I smiled. "I really don't mind cleaning up."

"Then what do you mind? You're not happy about something."

I shrugged. "I was kind of looking forward to riding."

"Then why aren't you going?"

"Well, you've got work to do."

"Yes, I've got work to do. What does that have to do with you?"

I put the dishes in the sink and sighed. "I work for you, Sid. If you've got notes to organize, then I'd better be here to help you with them."

"I didn't ask you to." Sid leaned against the sink with his arms folded.

"You don't get it, do you?" With a bitter smile, I turned on the water and waited for it to get hot. "You're the boss and a man to boot. I'm supposed to cater to your needs."

Sid thought. "I missed something."

"Oh. It figures." I squirted dish soap over the dishes and turned the faucet on them. "It's Mama. She wants me taking care of you instead of gallivanting all over the place on a horse. It really bugs her that you're her guest and you've been working at the store for us. Not that she's saying anything, of course. You just don't do that. But you sure catch hell if you don't pick up the code."

"I see." Sid finished clearing the table and picked up a towel. "I do want to get our interview notes outlined for the casino piece, maybe even go over the tape, but to be honest, I'd just as soon do it by myself. Not that you wouldn't be a help, but you hate that phase anyway."

"So I organize differently."

"Lisa, with all due respect, you are an excellent writer, but organizing it is not your strong suit."

"This is true. There's a typewriter in the living

room. I could start transcribing that tape."

"Why don't you go riding? You don't want to listen to an interview you've already done any more than I do. I'll get the notes organized, and then we can decide what we want to pull off the tape."

I smiled. "It's strange. I still feel guilty."

"I've been given to understand that's a common occurrence among people with parents." He smirked.

Once the kitchen was clean, I assuaged my conscience by getting Sid set up in the living room, then went in search of my riding boots.

Motley tagged along with me to the stables. Neff told me about this chestnut mare that Daddy had bought earlier that summer. She was a good, spirited mount, but not skittish. Motley barely got a nicker out of her. I was saddled up and trotting down a trail in no time.

I took the back way around to my by myself place. The mare was surefooted in the hills and Motley eagerly kept pace. He ran ahead as we neared the clearing, barking joyfully. I dismounted and led the mare through the trees.

Motley was busy sniffing out the whole clearing. Finally, he looked up and yipped disconsolately, as if he had expected to find something and hadn't. He put his nose to the ground and went over the clearing again.

I tethered my mount to a tree branch, stretched and went over to the boulder. The whole clearing was like a little promontory, with a sharp drop on all sides except where the trees backed into the hill. The valley sparkled below in the gray sunlight of a misty morning. White specks of light danced in the waves of the lake. Somewhere in the trees behind me, a blue jay raised cain.

Motley barked anxiously. I turned. The mare nickered and tossed her head, but stayed calm. Motley was barking at a bush near the edge of the clearing. Or, as I got a closer look, what had been a bush. Something or someone had squashed it flat. A little piece of fabric was caught in the thorns. I pulled it free. It was a piece of cotton flannel plaid in royal blue and black, part of one of a thousand shirts worn by locals and tourists alike.

But Motley was excited about it. I put the scrap in my pocket and made a mental note to ask Sid what Murray had been wearing when he was found. Taking one more look around, I went back to the horse and took her home by way of a good soft horse trail. It didn't take much to nudge her into a good spirited gallop, which Motley thoroughly enjoyed, too. I galloped her again on the cleared trail behind my parents' place, then cooled her down to a walk before I stabled her.

When I got back to the house, Sid had put the typewriter on the coffee table and was rattling away at lightning speed.

"Good lord," I gasped.

"Hm?" Sid looked up, then stopped the cassette player and removed the headphones. "Oh, you're back."

"May I ask why you are paying me to do your typing for you? You're a thousand times faster than I am."

"It is also one of my least favorite chores." Sid stretched. "Phew! You smell like horse. Why don't you clean up and we can get some work done? It'll save me from transcribing."

I laughed. "Then why are you doing it?"

"Nothing else to do," he said shrugging and replacing the headphones.

A second later, he was rattling away again. I took my time cleaning up mostly because I didn't want to get stuck transcribing. That has got to be the most mind-numbing job on the face of this earth. I had just finished changing when Mama knocked on my door.

"Sid told me he sent you riding this morning," she said coming in.

I towel dried my hair and fluffed it. "Yep."

"Did you have a good time?"

"Uh-huh. Took the new mare out. She's wonderful.

Where'd you guys find her?"

Mama laughed. "It's a long story. I'm glad you had a nice time."

"Yeah." I got my notebook out of my purse. "Did you want to chat?"

"Oh, no. You got work to do, honey. Here, let me take that towel and I'll put it in the hamper."

"Thanks." I hurried out to the living room.

"Lisle?" called Mama behind me. "Did you put your tack away?"

"Yes, Mama." I sighed as Sid shook his head. "I'll be seventy and she'll still be checking up on me."

Sid chuckled. "Which is precisely why I'm glad I got disowned. I can't imagine anything worse than perpetual childhood."

"Something tells me you were never a child."

Sid just grinned and continued typing, all the while humming "All Day, All Night Marianne." It's just about the only thing I've ever heard him sing and the only time he sings it is after he's been... [Doing it, humping, making the beast with two backs, getting it on, getting laid, screwing, fucking... Any others? - SEH]

"You've been here all morning, haven't you?" I whispered.

"Yes."

"You haven't been up to something, or should I say someone on the staff, have you?"

"No." He hadn't been.

I watched him type and hum some more.

"Must have been some night last night."

"Yeah." He sighed happily.

"You are so depraved."

"Ain't I, though." He typed another minute more, then removed the headphones. "Would you believe I got it all done?"

"You're kidding. There were three hours of interviews."

"That's about how long you were gone."

"I was not."

"Well, I scanned some of the unrelated stuff." He rolled the paper out of the typewriter and leaned back on the sofa. "Did you have a nice time?"

"I had a great time. Will we need this typewriter anymore? I'd like to put it away before somebody trips on the cord."

"Here, let me." Sid got up and grabbed it.

"Sid."

"I got it out. I can put it away." Which he did.

I shook my head. "It's my turn to be confused. Why are you being so helpful?"

"Aren't I normally?"

"Very helpful. It's just... You didn't have to help out at the store. Why did you?"

"I haven't the faintest idea, really." Sid looked at me and smiled. "It seemed better than sitting around watching you work, and there really wasn't anything else to do." He shrugged.

"I want you to know how much I appreciate it, and the transcribing, too."

"You're welcome. Shall we get some work done?"

I checked the front hallway. My mother was busy in the kitchen.

"I've got some other work for us to ponder." I pulled the scrap of cloth from my pocket.

"So?"

"Motley found it in this clearing I like. He was really excited about being there, and it suddenly dawned on me that Murray showed me the place originally. It's not a bad place for a secret rendezvous, even at night. It looks out over the valley. The trees screen any noise, and people can't see you from the trail. And it's only about a ten-minute walk from the nearest road."

Sid mused. "Less if you're driving."

"Not really. The trail's not wide enough for a four by four. You might make it on a dirt bike, but they're awful noisy for a secret meeting, and there are too many people around who would raise cain. I found the scrap in a bush that had been flattened, possibly by a fight.

Things looked a little scuffed up there. The question is, does that scrap match what Murray was wearing when you found him?"

"Nope. He had red and black on." Sid looked the scrap over. "This is not an unusual pattern."

"You said it." I took it back. "I would have written it off as a clumsy hiker except Motley was so wild about it. And it still doesn't answer anything about Della's killer."

"Somebody tall." Sid sat down in the easy chair and leaned back.

"Fletcher Haddock."

"That's right. He is." Sid mulled that over. "And if what you told me is true, he was very anxious to get into that suite."

I flopped onto the sofa. "That had nothing to do with Della."

"Maybe. Maybe not." Sid got up and prowled. "Young Lothario seems to be oddly persistent in his chase."

"I don't think it's so odd," I said, playing miffed. "Don't you think my own particular charm warrants that kind of fascination?"

"It does indeed." Sid smiled his little smile that never fails to stir me up. "But even I know when to quit trying."

I snorted. "If you've quit, I haven't noticed."

"You haven't given me the brush off. You did give it to Mr. Haddock in no uncertain terms, at least that's the impression I got."

"You got the right one." I noticed Sid watching me. "What are you looking at?"

"I have just now remembered that you do owe me something."

"Where did that come from?"

"Absolutely nowhere."

The next thing I knew, and I have no idea how he did it, I was on my back, pinned underneath him.

"Sid," I yelped. I started to tuck my feet under my

seat, but Sid's hand gently pushed them back down.

"No need for that," he said, mischief gleaming in his eyes.

"What are you doing?"

"Well, you were concerned about all the uncompensated work I did at your father's store, and there was a little something you more or less promised me Friday afternoon."

"What?"

His lips found mine in a sweet, warm, luscious, comfortable kiss. All too soon it was over.

"Oh, that," I whispered. I gazed into his eyes. "Is this your idea of getting even?"

His grin turned sly. "No. This is."

He moved fast, and before I could get my teeth closed, I was all but choking on his tongue. He knows I hate French kissing. It wasn't that bad, but I tucked my feet up under my seat to let him know he was going over if he kept it up any longer than I was willing to let him.

"What the hell is going on here?" Daddy's voice, thick with anger, split my ears.

I bucked. Sid went head first into the arm of the sofa, and as I tried to get as far away from him as possible, we both went over into the coffee table. Papers went flying. Sid got untangled first. I scrambled up, wiping my mouth, and faced my father.

"Nothing, Daddy," I said quickly.

"Nothing, my ass!" Daddy started towards Sid. "If I ever catch you-"

That did it.

"It doesn't make a damn bit of difference what you catch me doing," I yelled at Daddy, stepping in front of him. "In case you haven't noticed, I am over age. I am a full-grown woman, and I will do what I please, including work for Sid. It's my decision, not yours. And while I'm at it, will you get it through your thick skull that he is not going to rape or seduce me, and I am not sleeping with him, nor will I be sleeping with him unless we are married, which is pretty darned unlikely. I might also add that if I do decide to sleep with him, that is my decision, not yours. In fact, none of what I do with Sid is any of your business, so butt out!"

Daddy stood there, his mouth hanging open like a twenty-pound trout that couldn't believe it had gotten caught. I had never, ever, in my entire life, yelled at him like that. Unable to speak, he stumbled out of the living room. I fumed in the silence that followed.

"Thanks for defending me," said Sid finally.

I turned on him. "If you ever embarrass me like that in front of my family again, so help me, I'll-"

"Wait just one minute here." Sid glared at me. "Just because you're mad at your father is no reason to take it out on me."

"But I am mad at you, Sid. You should know better than to pull a stupid stunt like that."

"Aw, for crying out loud. We both knew it wasn't going anywhere. I thought we were past that nonsense."

"That nonsense has nothing to do with it. We are in my parents' house and my parents are here. Daddy doesn't like you as it is. Do you have to make it worse?"

"We were just rough housing."

"You know darned well what was going on on that sofa would not look like roughhousing to an uninformed spectator."

"I kissed you and he caught us. Big deal. As you pointed out, we are not horny teenagers. We are adults, and if he can't accept the fact that there's nothing going on between us, then it's his problem. Even if there was something going on, it's his problem."

"But, Sid..."

"Lisa, I have dealt with many, many irate fathers in my time. There isn't a thing you can do about them."

"You're not even trying."

"There is no point in trying. Don't you understand? As far as he's concerned, I am moving in on his little girl, and he's got to protect you. Men like that do not see reason."

"You don't have to write him off so quickly," I sobbed. "Can't you see how much your problem with him is hurting me?"

"Why? It has nothing to do with you, per se. It's between him and me."

"Didn't it ever occur to you that it tears me apart to see the two men I care about most in the world at each other's throats?"

Sid did the trout bit himself for a moment. I sniffed as the tears rolled down my cheeks.

"Do you really have that much invested in me?" he asked softly.

"Yes," I whispered, flushing.

He sighed and looked around the room with darting glances. His gaze finally fell on me, full of tenderness. He came over.

"Sid..." I backed up.

"I seriously doubt your father will come back in here any too soon."

"Probably not." I sniffed and laughed at the same time.

Sid pulled me into his arms and we held each other. He kissed my hair.

"Lisa, I am trying. But I can't change who I am, and that is the larger part of what your father finds fault with."

"Not really," I said and squeezed him. "He's never liked any male I've gotten close to. If you could just talk to him."

"I doubt he'd listen."

"He will. I asked him last night to talk to you. He said he would."

"Alright. I'll talk to him. But I'm not making any promises."

"Lisa, Sid. Oh!" Mama stopped in the doorway.

I pulled away quickly. "No, Mama. It's not what you think."

Sid bent and picked up the coffee table and the papers.

"I heard some yelling." Mama smiled, completely flustered. "And after what your Daddy said, Lisle, I..."

"We were just joking around," I said. "And Daddy took it wrong."

"Lisle, we'll talk about that later. Lunch is ready."

"Oh, good." Sid straightened.

We followed her into the kitchen.

"There's sandwiches on the table," said Mama.

"Thanks," said Sid, calm as ever.

Mama sighed. "Are you two alright?"

"Fear not, Althea. All is resolved." Sid sat down at a place setting and served himself.

"I just hope Lisa isn't in any trouble."

Sid laughed. "No, but I was for a few minutes there."

Mama did the trout bit.

"That was hardly the first fight we've had, Mama," I said, getting the milk out of the refrigerator.

"We fight all the time," said Sid. "And speaking of, that's not whole milk, is it?"

"Low fat," I shot back. "Think you can compromise for a change?"

Sid rolled his eyes. "I suppose I'll have to."

"Lisle," hissed my mother.

Sid caught it and grinned. "Relax, Althea. I am not going to fire your daughter for insubordination. Rather, I encourage it and the ongoing, if occasionally intense, open communication we enjoy."

"Where's Daddy?" I asked, trying to change the subject.

"He went back to the store after he ate." Mama glanced at Sid. "Like I said, Lisle, I want to talk to you about that later."

"Don't let me stop you," said Sid. "There's not much about your little girl I don't already know."

Mama laughed weakly. "I'm sure that's true, Sid, but I'd still prefer to talk to Lisa privately."

"Can I eat first?" I asked plaintively.

"Of course, honey." Mama smiled and shook her

head as I sat down and helped myself. "I know better than to keep you from your food. I swear, between you and your daddy, my food bill's been miserable. You know, Sid, when Mae moved out, the food bill stayed the same. When Lisa moved out, it dropped a full third."

"The dear girl has the appetite of a locust," Sid replied, smiling.

"She most certainly does." Mama gazed at the refrigerator. "She and her daddy have darned near emptied that already, and I filled it Monday. With Mae and Neil and the kids coming tomorrow, I'm going to have to go shopping this afternoon, and I've got cookies to bake for the kids."

"You want me to help, Mama?" I asked.

"Do I detect an ulterior motive?" Sid sniggered.

"Not originally," I replied. "But now that you mention it, I could see myself noshing on a little cookie dough. Maybe I'll go ahead and make my famous chocolate chip cookies."

"Ugh," said Sid.

"You might like these. I make them with whole wheat."

Sid shook his head. "No thanks. I never did like sweets."

"Lisle, if you don't mind coming to the grocery store with me, I'd like the company," said Mama. "That is, if Sid doesn't need you here."

"I don't know," said Sid thoughtfully. "Think you could handle my company also?"

"Oh, Sid, you don't have to," Mama said, glowing.

"Of course not. That's part of what makes it such a pleasure." He got up and picked up his empty plate and glass. "The other part is the pure joy of spending the afternoon under the influence of your maternal charm."

Mama laughed. "Young man, you and your snake oil. Now, here, let me take those."

"Nah. Got to pay my room and board somehow."

I hurried up and finished eating, and between the three of us, we had everything cleaned up in record time. In the meantime, Sid and Mama got into an extended discussion about menu planning. While food is one of my preferred topics, I much prefer eating it to talking about it. So as Sid and Mama put together the grocery list, I sat out on the back porch trying to piece things together. I didn't get very far.

The trip to the store was a lot of fun. Poor Mama is on Sid's side when it comes to healthy food, but she also likes indulging me when I'm home, so she made a point of distracting Sid several times while I stashed a few goodies in the basket. It was all but overflowing when we got to the check out counter.

"Well, hello, Althea." The blonde checker was overly made up and closer to my mother's age and had probably been at the store since she graduated from high school.

Sid perused the magazine rack at the end of the aisle.

"Howdy, Shireen. How are you?" Mama helped me empty the contents of the cart onto the conveyor.

Shireen looked at all the groceries. "Good heavens, Althea, what's all this for?" She noticed me and laughed. "Well, I'd heard Lisa was in town."

I flushed. Mama's smile grew tight.

"Mae and her family will be here, too," she said pleasantly. "They're coming for the weekend."

"How nice. Too bad about all that trouble you people are having." Shireen's fingers danced across the keys of the register. "All that business in Nevada, and now Murray. It sure is funny how Lisa's boss seems to be in the middle of it all." She glanced over at Sid, then lowered her voice. "Is that him?"

"Yes," said Mama.

"He is something." Shireen paused to look up the code for a bunch of kale, then gave me a meaningful look. "Almost makes you believe all the rumors."

"Shireen, he has been a perfect gentleman," said Mama, sounding cross. "It's all just jealous talk, and nothing more. And the police say the two murders might be connected, so it's no surprise Sid and Lisa have something to do with both of them."

Sid ambled up, reaching for his back pocket. "Althea, can-"

My foot put gentle, but obvious pressure on his. He looked at me funny for a second, but shut up. While Mama paid for the groceries, he dropped a ladies magazine on the conveyor belt. Shireen gave him a puzzled look.

"What's in that one?" I asked.

"The mutual funds how to." Sid got out his wallet. "I could use an extra set of tear sheets of that one."

"Is that one of the articles you wrote?" Mama asked.

"Yeah," said Sid.

"You really are a writer?" asked Shireen. "That'll be two dollars and seven cents."

Sid handed her a twenty. "Yep."

Shireen handed him his change with less lust and more admiration. Sid basically ignored her.

Mama was steaming by the time we all got back in the jeep. But Sid pulled out the magazine, which as he expected, got her interested in the article. It turned out she had the magazine at home and had even read the article and hadn't noticed who wrote it. Sid ribbed her gently about not reading by-lines, then confessed he didn't always pay attention either.

He also ribbed us about poisoning innocent children as we made cookies and refused to lift a finger to help.

"It goes against my morals," he explained.

"Since when do you have any?" I teased back.

"Lisle!" hissed Mama.

"Mama, I know Sid has morals," I said. "I was just teasing him because they're so different."

Mama sighed. "It doesn't make any difference to me what Sid's morals are. Some things you just don't talk about in mixed company. 'Tisn't nice."

Sid let out an exaggerated sigh. "Well, if we can't

talk about that, what will we talk about?"

Mama gasped, then laughed. "You are just terrible. I'm beginning to understand why Lisa yells at you."

Sid laughed himself and got the lettuce out of the refrigerator.

"May as well get the jump on dinner," he said. "What do you think about capers in the salad, too, Althea?"

Between the two of them, all I had to do was watch, which was fine with me. Daddy came in just after six. By that time dinner was ready, so he didn't notice that Sid had done as much of the cooking as Mama. The last thing we needed was for him to call Sid a sissy.

I was really nervous about Daddy, but he acted as if nothing had happened. He talked about the store and Les Stevens.

"Alice came in early, too," Daddy said as we finished eating.

"I wonder why," I said.

"Just trying to be helpful, I expect," said Daddy. "Practically took over the stock. Unpacked that whole shipment from yesterday and went through it extra careful."

"No kidding," said Sid. Our eyes met.

"Well, that was very nice of her," said Mama. "It's a good thing she's trying to get started right with Les. You know how fond she was of Murray. Of course, Murray was always good with teens. But Alice and him were real good friends."

"Really now," I said.

Sid and I glanced at each other. We both had a pretty good idea of what Alice had really been doing.

"So what all are we going to do tonight?" Mama asked, changing the subject.

Sid glanced at me. "Well, if it's alright with you, Bill, I'd like to leave the ladies to themselves and have a quiet chat with you."

Daddy looked at me, then Sid. "McKinley's bar alright?"

"Sounds fine to me," said Sid. "Tell you what. I'll buy the beer."

"Sounds like a plan."

They left right after dinner in the pickup truck.

"I hope it works," said Mama, stacking dirty dishes next to the sink.

"So do I." I grabbed the dishrag and wiped off the table.

"He was pretty upset by what you said to him this afternoon." Mama ran hot water into the sink. "I can't say he didn't deserve it, but I do wish you'd found another way to say it."

"He made me mad. I wish he could get it into his head that Sid and I are friends and that's all." I moodily tossed the rag into the sink. "I wish a lot of people would."

"Like Shireen." Mama set to washing the dishes.

"Yeah. Like Shireen. It was so obvious she thought Sid and I are... You know."

"Doing what married people do."

"Yeah." I got a towel and started drying. "They just can't believe that Sid and I are friends and that we don't have that kind of relationship. Maybe it's because we're so close. I can talk to Sid and just be myself in a way that I've never been able to before. It means a lot to me and it hurts when people insist on jumping to the wrong conclusion."

"Well, honey, people just don't understand that a man and a woman can have a real relationship without all that. It's a powerful urge."

"Believe me, I know, Mama." I dried a plate thoughtfully. "Mama? Do you and Daddy still..?"

"Still what, honey?"

"Still do what married people do?" I flushed. I don't know why I wanted to know. I guess it was all the snide comments Sid had made about my father, and I wasn't sure even if I did want to know.

Mama just smiled and glowed warmly. "Oh, of course. I don't think we'll ever stop. It just keeps getting better and better. That's because your daddy and I keep falling more and more in love with each other. I tell you, Lisle, when I first married your daddy, I didn't think I could love him any more than I did then. Now I know all I can do is love him more." She paused, then looked at me. "And I want to tell you, Lisle. I know of no greater pleasure than making love to your daddy."

"Oh." I quickly dried the plate again.

Mama laughed softly. "I didn't mean to embarrass you, honey. But I wanted you to know that. Married love is a very beautiful thing and I want you to have an idea of how beautiful it is for those times when you get tempted. And I know you do. It's only natural. Sid is a very attractive man. Lord knows, he even tempts me sometimes."

"He hasn't tried to..."

"No!" Mama went back to the dishes. "He's been a perfect gentleman."

"He'd better be."

"Of course, that's probably part of the attraction."

I did the trout bit. "Mama!"

We looked at each other, then burst into laughter.

We had finished cleaning up and were playing gin in the living room when the phone rang. Mama got up for it. The phone is in the hall next to the kitchen, so I couldn't hear anything. I leaned back on the sofa and scratched Motley. Murbles and Richmond came up for their share of the affection.

"Lisle," called Mama, hurrying in. "We've got to run. Sid and your daddy are in the middle of the biggest fight in years!"

"Oh my god!" I ran to my room and got my purse.

Mama had our coats in the front hallway. I dug for my keys as we ran out to the garage.

"I'll drive," I said, climbing behind the jeep's steering wheel. I had it started before Mama was settled in her seat.

"I just can't figure out what went wrong," groaned Mama as I backed down the driveway.

"I have no idea. Sid just isn't going to get violent unless he's attacked."

"Your daddy's not going start anything unless he really lost his temper. I hope he's not hurting Sid too badly."

"I doubt it." I shuddered. "Sid's probably hurting him. He's a lot tougher than he looks. Oh no. Maybe Daddy called him gay. Sid really doesn't like it when a straight calls him gay."

"Well, he knows Sid isn't. Landsakes, with the way people have been talking, it's only obvious.

"I don't know what else could have started it unless Sid got crass and that's what made Daddy mad."

"I don't know, honey."

[I will now interject my recollection of what occurred at the bar. Neither the talk, or what happened afterwards, will soon be forgotten.

"Bottle or draft?" I asked Bill as we went in.

There was an awkward pause as Bill looked me over. We hadn't really said anything on the way over beyond the usual trite observations on the weather. The bartender settled it.

"Howdy, Bill," he called and waved. "Guinness Stout?"

"Yep."

"What's your friend having?" The bartender gave me a shrewd once over. "Corona with lime?"

The regulars sitting at the bar watched. In fact, almost everyone in the room had their eyes on me one way or another. It wasn't all that bad a guess, but I was not in a yuppy mood that night.

I shook my head. "You got Harp?"

The bartender looked surprised. "Afraid not."

"Guinness Stout, then."

"It's bottled."

"What's on tap?"

"Bud."

I stifled the gag. "Stout, please. I'm buying for the two of us."

Bill went off and found us a table in a quiet corner. The bartender got out the two bottles and a pair of mugs then took my money. I left a good tip in consolation. The regulars shook their heads and muttered amongst themselves. One young fellow went straight for the phone.

"Where'd you pick up a taste for Guinness?" I asked Bill as I sat down.

"Malcolm O'Malley." Bill poured along the side of the glass. "Neil's daddy. We were friends in college. Malcolm's got family in England."

I nodded. I poured my stout trying to find the right words to say. Strangely enough, I wasn't getting much from Bill. (What's strange about that? Daddy never was one to volunteer anything – ljw)

"Look, Bill," I said slowly. "I realize there are a few differences in our respective philosophies and values. But I'd like to come to some sort of an understanding, seeing as though it looks like we're going to be thrown together periodically. For Lisa's sake."

He glared at me. I went back over my words, wondering what the hell I'd said. He noticed.

"I guess you don't realize, I had a talk like this with Neil some years back," he growled. "And he started it just about the same way. Two days later, he and Mae were engaged."

I laughed. "That is not going to happen, Bill. Lisa was telling the truth. There is nothing going on between us, at least nothing she doesn't think should be."

"What about you?"

I chose my words carefully. "Well, you have to understand, I was raised very differently than most people. I was taught that there's nothing wrong with sex, or that it should be limited to any special context beyond free consent. I was also taught that marriage is a lie. Now I know you and Lisa don't agree. I respect that. I just ask that you give me the same respect."

"I'll admit I'm a little worried about yours, but it ain't values." Bill sighed. "I don't suppose you know much about being a father."

"I, uh, made a point of surgically preventing that possibility some years ago."

Bill nodded. "That would be the smart thing to do. What do you see when you look at Lisa?"

"I see a remarkable, talented, beautiful woman. She's very caring, very efficient. I don't mind admitting I'm very fond of her."

"But you see her as a woman."

"She is."

Bill sighed. "She is at that, and a fine one, too. But when I look at her, I see a whole lot more than you ever could. I see a sixteen-year-old girl crying because she just missed getting on the pep squad. I see her heartbroken when some boyfriend of hers would break up with her and forget to tell her. I see a twelve-year-old girl who was up half the night working on a composition, making it the very best she could to impress her English teacher. He told her it weren't worth bothering with in front of the whole class. I remember a little six-year-old girl who didn't understand why she couldn't go out and play with the other children because she was still pretty sick and we couldn't let her catch cold. Then there was the double pneumonia when she was seven. And when she was born, I'd wanted a boy. Told all my friends and relatives I was going to have a son. But when I saw her in that incubator, she was so tiny, only four and a half pounds, she was premature, you know. She weren't supposed to make it. I tell you, Sid, there's no worse feeling than watching your child suffer and knowing there ain't a damn thing you can do to stop it." Bill took a deep pull on his stout. "She's been hurt so many times by boys that only wanted her body."

"I value her for far, far more than that."

"I suppose." He glared at me again. "But you got the best shot at hurting her."

"I'd never do that, at least not consciously."

"It's the unconscious part that bothers me. Believe me, I know how it could happen. You get close. You get the itch and catch her off guard."

I chuckled to cover my discomfort. "We are very aware of that possibility. Nothing's happened, and I don't think it will. I won't lie to you, Bill. I would very much like to make love to her, and if the time ever comes when she can freely give herself to me without any guilt feelings, I will not refuse her. But the key word is freely. She can't now and maybe never will, and that's fine with me. I'm very happy with the way things stand right now. That may surprise you. It sure as hell surprises me."

"You ever think about marrying her?"

"Not really. She has told me that's the only acceptable way for us to make love, but I can't make that kind of commitment to her. She expects fidelity, which is fine for her, but I feel is a little unrealistic. Like I said, I was raised with the idea that marriage is a lie. And to be honest, I don't think she really wants to make that commitment to me or anybody. She's very content as a single person. She values her independence."

Bill laughed quietly. "She always was her own woman, just like her mama."

"And like her father?"

"Nah." He shook his head. "I'm just bull-headed." He sighed then looked at me. "I can't say that I'll ever stop worrying about you."

I nodded. "That's fair, I suppose, since I'm not about to marry Lisa."

"Who said I stopped worrying about Neil?"

"You two get along really well."

He shrugged. "I just got used to him."

I had to laugh and lifted my mug. "Here's to getting used to each other, no matter how long it takes."

We clinked glasses and drank. Bill finished his off. There was some commotion at the door as six young toughs came in. Bill ignored them.

"What say I buy the next round," he said.

"Sure. Thanks."

However, before he could get up, the toughs came over, led by a punk in his early twenties, if that old. He was scrawny, with bushy brown hair, a red nose that ran, and an anxious look in his eyes. Antsy is the only way to describe his movements, his whole demeanor.

"You Sid Hackbirn?" he demanded, his voice just barely in control.

"Yes," I replied, regretting Bill's presence. I had my twenty-two on my shin, but using it would raise too many questions.

"What do you want, Donny Severn?" Bill asked, also on guard.

"He's been fucking my girl!" Donny's voice cracked.

"Have you?" Bill watched me, wondering.

I shrugged. "It's possible. I've gotten quite a few offers, and if a woman is offering herself to me, then I assume it's her responsibility if she's in a relationship with someone else, and I don't ask if she is."

"I knew it!" Donny lunged at me.

Bill put his hand up and stopped him, then glared at me.

"Do you ask how old she is?" he asked.

"If there's any doubt, I'll card her." I looked at Donny, wondering. "What's your girlfriend's name?"

"I don't have to tell you shit, fuckface."

I looked at Bill. "I did card Alice Martin."

"You fuck!" Donny lunged again. "You did it! Admit it. You did it!"

Donny's friends held him back that time.

I laughed. "If you think I fell for that phony ID, think again."

"You lie. She said you did. She said you raped her in the back room."

"I never touched her. Sorry, Donny, but it wasn't me."

Donny burst forward and got a hold of my shirt, swearing with a remarkably limited vocabulary. I rose as he pulled me up, then grabbed his wrists and pulled them from my shirt. He was taller than me by at least six inches, and also had the reach to go with it. Even if he wasn't all there mentally, that antsy, almost manic, mood of his made him exceptionally dangerous.

"I am not a violent man," I said, giving him a small shove backwards. "But do not do that again."

Stevie Wonder could have seen Donny's swing coming. I wondered if I should deck him, then decided to catch his hand instead. I dug my fingers into the tendons on top of his wrist. Donny winced and yanked himself free.

"You prick!" he yelled, backing into his friends. "Next time stick to fucking Lisa Wycherly. Or isn't her cunt good enough? Is that why you fuck everyone else?"

Bill started out of his seat.

"Bill, I'll take care of this." I walked over to Donny, got my fingers in his hair, and slowly pulled his face down to mine. "If you want to pick a fight with me, then so be it. But leave Miss Wycherly out. Is that clear?"

Donny trembled and nodded. I shoved him into his friends and turned my back. I heard Donny coming. It was always possible he had a knife, so I swung around and put my elbow into his jaw. The knife dropped from his hand and slid under a table. Anger rippled through the five other toughs like a fire through brush. As Donny staggered back, they rushed me only to find that Bill was there, too. The fight was on - SEH]

A crowd had gathered at the door of the bar. Mama and I pushed our way through. All of a sudden, everyone backed away from the center of the fight.

"He's got a knife!" someone screamed.

"Where'd that come from?" yelped someone else.

"Under the table," replied a calmer voice.

I nearly landed on my face when I finally got through to the front. Donny Severn slashed at Sid, who dodged. The two circled each other. Sid's eyes were fixed on Donny's shoulders, watching for the next lunge. Donny feinted, then slashed the other way. Sid rolled, then bounced back as Donny recovered. I crossed myself on reflex.

Moisture shone on Sid's forehead, but it was nothing compared to the sweat Donny had broken. Drops of perspiration flew as Donny lunged again, just barely missing. Another drop wiggled from the end of Donny's red nose. Donny charged and the drop broke loose. Sid rolled away. They squared off again.

Donny feinted then slashed. Sid was ready and waiting. He rolled, then caught Donny's knife hand. But Donny was wild and struggled hard. Sid clamped his other hand around Donny's wrist, trying to force the knife free. He backed into Donny, who dropped his free arm around Sid's neck and forced the point of the knife towards Sid's belly. The two strained until Sid slammed his foot onto Donny's.

Donny howled. Within seconds, Sid had forced the knife free. He whipped around and put Donny out for the count with a strong left in Donny's ear.

"Bill!" Mama cried.

She ran over to where Daddy stood gasping. He wiped his mouth with the back of his hand, and I just barely noticed the dark stain. Sid, gasping, leaned his head back for a moment, then staggered towards Daddy. Blood dripped from his nose. Behind me, I could hear the police fighting their way through the crowd.

Daddy met Sid in the center of the room and shook his hand. Then he leaned on Sid's shoulder and doubled over, hugging his aching ribs.

Daddy is not a brawler, but this wasn't the first time he'd been caught in a fight. With him being so large and keeping himself up like he does, there are those who think it's fun to take him on. The police officers knew Daddy, and there were plenty of witnesses happily swearing that Donny and his friends had started all the trouble and that Daddy and Sid were only fighting in self-defense. Not that witnesses were needed. The officers were perfectly happy to bust Severn and company.

Mama got Daddy into the truck, while I took Sid back in the jeep. We put them in the kitchen and tended to the wounds there.

"You boys ought to be ashamed of yourselves," said Mama, as she wrapped Daddy's chest with an ace bandage. "I don't care what everyone was saying, there had to be a peaceful way of settling things."

"And I tried every one," said Sid.

He winced as I cleaned around his rapidly swelling left eye.

"Did you lose your contact lens?" I asked.

"Nope."

"That Donny Severn's just a hothead," grumbled Daddy.

"He's more than that," said Sid. "Unless I miss my guess, he's hooked on coke."

"Coke?" asked Mama. "I suppose you could be, but soda pop sure seems like a funny thing to be addicted to."

"Mama," I groaned, dropping ice cubes into a plastic bag. "Cocaine."

"Oh, landsakes! What was I thinking of?" Mama paused. "But Sid, what makes you think that?"

I tied the plastic bag shut and wrapped it in a towel.

"His nice red nose and chronic sinus condition," Sid replied casually, as he let me lay the improvised ice bag on his eye.

"That could be just a cold," said Mama.

"Not really," said Sid. "He was too antsy and anxious for a fight."

"Well, you fixed him," Daddy chuckled. "Would you believe, Althea, the wimp throws one hell of a punch."

He does, too, and I know from personal experience. We were working out together one morning at the martial arts dojo we go to and Sid accidentally clipped me in the head. It felt roughly like being hit by a truck.

"Feeling dizzy?" I asked him softly.

"Not at all."

"You hurt anyplace else?"

"Nope. Got it all in my face."

"Bill always gets it in the chest," said Mama. "That's because he's so tall."

Finished with Daddy, she began picking up. I helped Sid out of the chair, and put my arm around his shoulders.

"I'm alright," he grumbled, trying to pull away. "I can walk by myself."

"You don't have to," I snipped. "So don't."

He gave in and I helped him into his room and shut the door as he eased himself onto the bed.

"Your observation regarding Donny is pretty interesting," I said quietly.

"Indeed, it is." Sid nodded. "Especially when you consider he's very close to Alice."

"He is?"

"There's apparently some sort of relationship. That's what the whole brouhaha was about. Alice had told him I'd practically raped her in the back room of the store and he was there to avenge her honor."

"Curiouser and curiouser."

"You said it."

"But where does Donny fit in?"

Sid shrugged as well as he could. "I wish I knew. I'd really like to talk to him."

"Unless you've decided to blow our cover, that will not be easy."

"We'll see." Sid mused. "There are ways."

I nodded. "I'll bet. By the way, did you and Daddy get a chance to talk?"

"We even achieved a truce of sorts." He smiled at me. "Your father is naturally worried because he can't keep you safe in the fold, and as far as I'm concerned, he's fully aware of the potential for disaster. In a way, I know how he feels."

"What do you mean?"

"How many times have I had to come to your rescue when your date got fresh and you ditched him?"

I blushed. "Not that many."

"But, Lisa, you are very good at getting yourself

in over your head." He smiled and reached out for my hand. I gave it to him and he squeezed it gently.

"You know me," I said awkwardly. "I trust people, that's all."

"I know." Sid sighed. "In some ways, I'd rather you didn't. But you trusted me, and it's made all the difference." He looked away sadly.

"What's wrong?"

His gaze settled on me. "I was just thinking about the fight."

I nodded. "I thought I heard Daddy mumble something Severn talking dirty and you defending my honor. What was that all about?"

"That." Grunting, Sid got up. "Severn just had a few nasty things to say and I let him know I was not going to tolerate it."

"Is that when you hit him?"

"No. I waited until he attacked me."

"Oh." I sighed and looked away.

"What's the matter?"

"Nothing. I just... I was wondering if you were standing up for me to impress Daddy."

Sid smiled and put his hands on my shoulders. "For all I want to make peace, I'm not going to start a barroom brawl to impress your father. Severn's remarks were grossly inaccurate, and while I did not want to fight him, I was not about to let them pass." He looked into my eyes, his own bright blue ones full of warmth. "Lisa, I have a lot invested in you, too."

I smiled, my heart pounding. "Thanks. I needed to hear that."

He gave me a quick hug and released me. "Goodnight, Lisa."

"Goodnight, Sid."

September 22, 1983

"What are you two all dressed up for?" Mama asked as Sid and I came into the kitchen for breakfast that morning.

We were both in standard business wear. Before that we'd been running, as usual, in spite of the previous night's wounds. Sid was pretty much recovered, except for a spectacular shiner on his left eye. He had wanted me to shower first, which is why we appeared together.

"We've got some research we've got to double check," said Sid. "In fact, we may want to eat in the car."

"But it's so early," Mama said.

It was almost seven thirty.

"That's the way it goes sometimes," said Sid.

I took the pile of toast and some paper towels and we were on our way. I thought Sid was being a bit over cautious regarding the time. But it's true that as soon as you assume the precautions aren't needed, that's when you wish you'd taken them.

Sid parked the 450 SL across the street at the bottom of the driveway leading up the hill to South Lake Tahoe High School. Teenagers came from all directions, in packs, pairs and singly, laughing, solemn, all trudging up the hill.

"So, that's the old alma mater," said Sid gazing up at what could be seen of the school.

"Yep. Where I spent four of the most miserable years of my life."

Sid looked over at me. "Were they really that bad?"

"I don't know." I shrugged. "There were high spots. I don't think I was chronically unhappy, although it seemed like I cried my way through junior year. I just didn't fit in the whole time I was there. I had friends, like Jimmy, but except for Leslie, they were never that close. It's not a time of my life I'd like to re-live."

"Adolescence can be difficult." Sid gazed out at the students. "I used to think I had a rough time of it. Then they sent me to 'Nam. Kind of put a new perspective on the whole thing. And as time goes by, the bad stuff seems to fade away, and all I can remember are the good times." Sid looked over at me. "Maybe I'll take you by the old school someday. You might like it, after all the fuss you made over my yearbooks."

I snorted. "I only fussed because you made such a fuss about not showing them to me."

"I do not make fusses. However, you get embarrassed easily and I didn't think you'd appreciate some of the inscriptions the old gang left behind."

"I didn't even look at them. I knew what your friends were like." I looked him over. "I know I'm sure to regret asking, but most likely to what?"

"Oh. You mean me and Liz Warner?"

"Yeah. You were voted most likely to, and it never said what."

Sid laughed. "That was the idea. You supplied your own. It was my buddy, Tom Freeman's idea. He was the yearbook editor."

"Didn't he beat you up when you were a freshman?"

"He got over it, especially when he realized being my friend made it a lot easier for him to get laid. Anyway, he decided that someone as notorious as I was deserved some sort of recognition, and since they couldn't print my homecoming record."

"Why not?"

Sid chuckled lecherously. "It was an underground thing. They even had it going long before I got there. We always had our Homecoming game on Friday and the dance on Saturday. After the game, the cheerleaders would throw this huge party, and the guys would see how many girls they could each lay in one night."

"And you hold the record."

"World champeen and still undefeated at sixteen

females."

"Must have been a small party. I would have thought you'd done it with twenty or twenty-five."

Sid choked. "When I think of how I nearly killed myself that night."

I flushed. "Is it that hard to do it that many times in one night?"

"It's impossible. Males have to recharge, you know. Your average teenage male can get it up again faster than an adult, but even then, four times in six to eight hours is asking a lot. I once pushed it to five times in one eight-hour period, but that last time wasn't easy."

"Then how did you get sixteen?"

"Nobody said I had to complete the act. I just had to penetrate." Sid chuckled. "Della and I did get a chance to gossip. She told me Tom is teaching there now. Apparently, he's been there something like six years. She ran into him last June at some conference or other. Tom told her my old record still stands. When he first got there, it was considered a myth until Tom set them straight. But they have yet to figure out how I did it."

"Didn't Tom tell them?"

Sid laughed. "Tom's lucky he can remember being there. He got exceptionally stoned that night, even for him."

"There she is." I pointed out the window.

The flow of students had slowed to a trickle. Alice Martin walked with two other girls, the three of them giggling and smoking cigarettes. Sid glanced at the dashboard clock and shook his head.

"Late, late, late," he said. "And before you say you told me so, you told me so."

"But like you said, it wasn't worth taking the chance." I put my hand on the door.

Sid held up his hand. We waited until they were almost past us before we got out of the car. We walked up behind the three girls.

"Good morning, Alice," Sid said loudly.

She froze and her friends stopped. Sid wandered around and sandwiched her between himself and me.

"Oh, hi," she said nervously.

Sid looked at her girlfriends. "Would you ladies mind if Alice and I had a private chat?"

The two girls took off running. Alice trembled.

"Please don't kill me," she cried. "I didn't sic Donny on you, honest! It was, like, his idea. I totally tried to stop him."

"You could have told him the truth," said Sid.

"Well, I– I tried. Honest. But he didn't believe me, and... And he's been running around on me. Like, I know it. He said he was in Reno, but I called his friend, Mike, Friday night and Mike said he wasn't there, said Donny was staying with him but he was, like, out all the time. He was with some other girl. I know he was. And... And that's why I said you and me did it." Alice sniffed and got a grip on herself. "I told him it was totally hot, like we were all over the place, and screaming and everything." She caved in. "I just, like, wanted to make him jealous. I didn't think he'd go after you. I really didn't."

"I realize having an unfaithful lover can be a painful experience," said Sid. "However, there are many more mature ways to deal with it. And right now, what I want to deal with is Murray."

"Murray?" Alice looked at him, puzzled.

"Yeah. I've got reason to believe someone is about to pin a bum rap on me, and I want to make sure he doesn't. What do you know about any side businesses Murray had?"

Alice almost backed into me. "Uh. Uh. Side businesses?"

"So there is one." Sid moved in closer. "Why don't you just tell me about it up front?"

"I don't know anything about that."

"You don't?" Sid asked, oh so innocently. "I just can't help wondering if it might have something to do with why Donny's nose is so red. And why you've been so extraordinarily helpful in the stockroom this past week. What's in the stock, Alice, that you don't want Bill Wycherly to find? The books are okay, so it isn't money. It's got to be something illegal."

"Like, why should I tell you?"

"Because if you don't, I'm going to tell the police that you know what's going on at Wycherly's store. And then they'll start looking, which will make whoever it is that doesn't want anybody to know what's going on very angry, and probably very angry at you for telling, and two people have already died over this."

"Oh." Alice trembled.

"You know," I said. "If you tell us, we can tell the police that you cooperated, and they can protect you."

"But I didn't do anything," Alice sobbed. "I just knew about it. It was Murray. He was, like, dealing coke. He said Lehrer made him do it. The coke came in the Sunland Products stuff. It was mostly back orders. Murray gave it to Lehrer. Only, like, last Friday, the stuff hadn't come in. It was supposed to come in Thursday night, but it didn't."

I put my arm around her shoulders. "Are you afraid Lehrer killed Murray?"

"I don't know what to think about that," cried Alice. "Cause... Cause a week ago, last Wednesday night, Murray stayed late with me. He did that, you know. Anyway, Lehrer came in, and they went in the stockroom, but it was slow, so I could like listen, and Lehrer said he'd turn Murray in if Murray didn't do a job for him, or get someone who could. And Donny came in and wanted his stuff, but Murray wouldn't give it to him unless he did Lehrer's job. So, Donny went off with Lehrer. But that's all I know. I swear it, on a stack of bibles."

I looked over at Sid. "What about another guy, a marketing guy from High Wilderness?"

Alice brightened. "Fletcher Haddock. He's been around lots. Your dad really likes him." She made a face. "Well, he used to like him. It's like totally weird.

Fletcher was in all afternoon yesterday with Les and your dad, only your dad was like totally teed off at Fletcher. Wouldn't talk to him, and kept giving him these totally mean looks."

Sid glanced at me. "Alright, Alice. Thanks for being straight with us. We'll keep you out of it, and make sure you have protection. We promise."

Alice nodded.

"Of course, if Lehrer or anyone else finds out you've been talking to us, all promises are off. You do understand that, don't you?"

Terrified, Alice nodded. We sent her on her way and went back to the car. Sid waited before starting the engine.

"If Lehrer's running coke," I mused aloud. "Then did he kill Della?"

"I don't think he did the actual killing," said Sid. "Why, when he had Donny to do it for him?"

"And Donny fits the tall and skinny description."

"Indeed, he does. But all we've got is the word of one scared teenager." Sid started the engine.

"And what about Lehrer and Murray?"

"That, too, is a good question."

We went to the South Lake Tahoe police station. Donny wasn't there, or in the local jail, either.

"He made bail," Officer Burke told us. "Though just between you and me and the lamppost, he would have been better off sticking around. That kid should have been in the hospital."

"Was he that badly hurt?" I gasped.

"Not by that fight. A patrol unit caught him staggering around near the Heavenly ski lifts Tuesday night, actually, Wednesday morning by that point. Somebody had roughed him up, but he either didn't know who or didn't want to say. He refused treatment at the emergency room and we had to release him."

"Too bad," said Sid. "I was hoping to talk to him. Clear the air and all."

"He's probably back in Reno," said Burke with a

disgusted look.

"Family?" asked Sid.

"Nah. Friends. He was there all weekend according to them, since the Wednesday before. We were looking at him for the Waters killing. Found his prints all over this one shelf in the stockroom." Burke glared at us. "Under all of yours, by the way."

"We didn't know," I said.

Burke cracked a smile. "Figures. But he had reason to be around, with that Martin kid his girlfriend and all, and no telling when he put the prints there."

"How tight was his alibi?" asked Sid casually.

"Tight enough. He was staying with a Mike Stripkin while he was there, and was in and out. Stripkin says he was there at the critical time. And there were other friends who vouched for him, just enough to be trustworthy."

"Do they know what actually killed Murray?" I asked.

"A blow to the head. We're not sure with what. Coroner said it could have been a gun butt, but why hit someone when you can shoot them?"

"True," said Sid. "Well, thanks a lot for your time."

I waited until we were outside. "There are a couple good reasons for hitting someone with a gun instead of shooting them."

"Such as?" Sid held the door open for me.

I waited until he was in his seat. "You're out of bullets, or you don't want someone to hear the shot, or you weren't trying to kill the person, just knock him out."

Sid nodded. "Makes sense. But it doesn't say whodunnit yet, and now that Donny has an alibi, he's out of the running."

"True. Not to mention we're still in the dark regarding the location of the agent we're looking for." I sat back and frowned. "You know, Sid, if we assume the cocaine was the motive behind Della's death, then what Tom Collins said about her death being related to the secrets is completely off, and we have nowhere to look for the secrets."

"Except Sunland Products. Remember, the secrets were traced to them somehow."

"I wonder if there's been a mistake. Maybe someone thought what they saw were secrets when it was cocaine being smuggled. Then again, there's the Company interest in Lehrer."

Sid pulled out his pocket watch. "That is interesting, but since we know Lehrer is dealing, that could be just drug related." The music tinkled out, then stopped. Sid started the engine. "We do have a second interview to conduct. Let's go."

The interview cleared up some points for the article but did nothing to illuminate the case. We got out of there by eleven.

"So where to now?" I asked as we got back in the car.

"Your folks' place." Sid started the engine and brightened. "Mae and Neil and company should be there by now."

I grinned. "Wait. We've got to stop at the grocery store."

"For what?"

"I've got to get some candy for the kids. I always have it for them. They'll be disappointed."

Sid glared at me briefly. "As much as I do not want to disappoint the children, you are not going to manipulate me into doing something that goes against my principles."

"Please, Sid?" I blinked twice, only he wasn't looking. [Are you kidding? I was not about to take a chance on getting suckered by those gorgeous cow eyes of yours. I kept my eyes glued to the road for my own well-being and that of the children - SEH]

Sure enough, as we pulled into the parking lot, Mae and Neil's station wagon was there.

Now, Mae is six years older than me and short, like Mama, but with a little padding. She wears her brown hair short and curly and out of the way. Neil is about two years older than Mae, and her opposite in stature. Tall and spare, his hair is bright red and he wears wire-rimmed glasses with thick lenses. Nothing ever seems to phase him. He's incredibly easy going, which is probably how he survives with five very bright, very active children.

The oldest is Darby, a red head and out and out skinny. He also has his father's poor eyesight. He was ten and a half at the time and a pretty good guitarist.

Marty and Mitch, the twins, are the youngest. They were three, and though they don't wear glasses yet, given how much they take after Darby and Neil, it's a safe bet they'll be wearing them. Given their hyperactive tendencies, Mae's not looking forward to it.

Ellen was five at the time. A brunette with her father's blue eyes, she's the shy one of the group, happiest when left to herself. Unfortunately, that usually results in a large mess of some sort because Ellen is insatiably curious, too.

Then there's Janey. She was seven at the time. Her hair is brown and she has big round hazel cow eyes. That's only a small part of the reason she's Sid's favorite. She's a very loving, sweet little girl with an incredible gift for character analysis. Her rating system is pretty simple: people are either good or bad. Sid is a good person. He just does bad things. But Janey loves him wholeheartedly nonetheless, and he is completely besotted with her. It's almost a joke, but if the kids want something from Uncle Sid, they know all they have to do is get Janey to ask.

The kids came running out of the house as soon as Sid stopped the engine. It was one noisy melee, with the three dogs running around barking and the kids yelling. Darby shook Sid's hand. Ellen attached herself to Sid's leg. The twins demanded their hugs and kisses. Sid bent to their demands. Janey waited as Marty and Mitch quickly bussed Sid's cheek and went running off, then she ran into his arms for her own special hug and kiss.

"How's my best girlfriend?" Sid asked her fondly while I distributed hugs and kisses to the rest of the brood.

"Real good, Uncle Sid." She looked at his shiner with a worried frown. "You got hurt."

"It's not bad at all."

Janey gently kissed the black eye. "There. That'll make it all better."

"It just might." Sid laughed and straightened.

Ellen tugged shyly on his sleeve and whispered.

"I'm sorry, Ellen, I didn't hear you," said Sid.

"Ellen, you got to talk louder," said Janey.

Ellen hollered, "I lost my first tooth!"

"Let's see," said Sid. Ellen opened her fist. "That's nice, but where did it come from?"

Laughing, Ellen opened her mouth and showed us the gap in her lower jaw.

"It's been loose for weeks and weeks," said Janey. "And Darby pulled it this morning in the car, but Daddy said it was s'posed to come out on its own, but Darby pulled it anyway."

"I'm glad," said Ellen emphatically. "I wanted it out."

"I'm getting another loose tooth," said Janey. She had gaps on either side of her permanent front teeth as it was, and she wiggled her right eye tooth.

"Tooth fairy's coming tonight," said Ellen softly, and she tugged on Sid's sleeve again. "Uncle Sid, does she know I'm at Grandma's?"

"I don't see why not." Sid glanced at me for help. "I'm sure she's got excellent radar."

"Lisa, Sid," called Mama from the porch. "Hurry on in. Mae and Neil want to say hi and we just got the photo box out."

The kids cheered and ran into the house with Mama following.

"Photo box?" Sid asked.

I grimaced. "All the family photos. Mama keeps

them in this huge gift box. The first thing Mae does when she visits is get the darned thing out. If I didn't have to go say hello."

"Why do I sense more ambivalence than boredom from you?" Sid's eyes twinkled.

"Maybe because that's what I'm feeling." I sighed. "I don't know. My early pictures aren't so bad, but sometime in junior high school, my face got long, and I just haven't taken a decent photograph since."

"That's not true." Sid gave my shoulders an affectionate squeeze. "It'll be okay. I'm beginning to get interested."

I glared. "My dearest reprobate, if you even think about laughing or making any snide comments, I promise you will regret it for the rest of your born days."

Sid just laughed.

We hello'd and hugged and kissed everyone, and Sid got maneuvered to the sofa between Mama and Mae. While that was going on, I quickly pawed through the box, looking for a specific set of pictures that under no circumstances did I want Sid to see. They weren't there, so I got a magazine and sulked in a chair across the room.

Sid smiled at all the pictures, although the rat seemed really interested in the ones of me. The kids wandered in and out. The twins were mostly out, supposedly playing in the kitchen. Janey suddenly tackled Daddy and away they went. Neil plopped down on the floor next to me.

"Your mom says things have been pretty rough for you up here," he said with a grin.

I shrugged. "There's not much we can do about it. I'd really rather not talk about it, if you don't mind."

Neil nodded at the group on the sofa. "Pretty boring, huh?"

"You said it." I put down the magazine. "Why is Mae so hung up those stupid things? It's not like she hasn't seen them a thousand times already."

"I don't know." Neil shook his head. "She's just as bad about the kids' baby pictures, and we've got them on the walls at home. She has got a new audience for a change."

Sid was examining one of the older photos. I could tell because the edge was crinkle cut. He looked over at me.

"Good lord, you were small as a baby," he said.

"Which one is that?" I asked.

He held it up. It's a picture of me at one month old, fresh home from the hospital. Daddy's sitting in a big armchair, with Mae hanging over the arm. Daddy's holding me and they're both looking at me, only it's pretty hard to see me for the receiving blanket. Well, I couldn't have been much bigger than six pounds at that point. Sid looked at it fondly and blushing, I turned back to my magazine.

Mama bounced up. "Oh, Lisle, I was cleaning out the closets before we went to Yellowstone, and look what I finally found."

She got the four books from the cupboard next to the bookshelf.

"Uh, Mama, why don't I take those?" I got up and snagged them. "It's kind of silly for you to be keeping them for me, anyway."

"Well, honey, I like looking at your yearbooks."

Sid's eyebrow lifted. "Yearbooks, huh?"

I glared at him. But I knew he'd be going through them sooner or later. Obviously losing them in the bottom of my former closet hadn't worked.

"And would you believe, I finally found your prom pictures." Mama handed the five by seven brown cover to Sid.

"No!" I yelped, diving for them.

I was too late. Sid held his laughter in like a gentleman, but I could see him shaking with the effort. He handed the folder back to me.

"What were you on?" he asked softly.

"I just blinked wrong."

"And the dreamboat you were with..?"

"Now, Michael was very nice," said Mama. "Lisa's just fussed because I talked her into taking him to the Christmas Dance, and when he asked her to the prom, she felt she had to go with him."

"They weren't exactly lining up to take me," I grumbled bitterly.

"I thought Michael was very sweet," said Mama.

"Very, very sweet," I said. "He took me to the prom because he wanted to go and couldn't take his boyfriend."

"Michael Tipton was gay?" asked Mae.

"Is gay," I corrected.

"Now, Lisa, you don't know that," said Mama.

"I met him down at Cal State, Mama. We both went there. He was president of the Gay and Lesbian Student Union." And I left the room before Mama could say anything else.

I found myself in the kitchen and got an apple out of the refrigerator. The windows over the back porch were open and I could hear Daddy and Janey talking.

"You just have to share," she told him. "That's all, Grandpa."

He laughed softly. "It's not that simple, sugarplum."

"It is so. And Uncle Sid isn't a bad person."

"I never said he was."

"You've been awful mean to him."

"We've been talking."

"You still don't like him."

"I worry about him, that's all. About grown up stuff, and never you mind about it."

"Oh, Grandpa. I'm not a little kid anymore. I know Uncle Sid has sex with his girlfriends. Can we go look at the horses?"

I was choking, first with laughter at Janey not being a little kid, and then over what she said about Sid. Mae came in.

"There you are," she said.

"Janey's on to Sid," I whispered, although Janey

and Daddy had long since left.

"What?" asked Mae.

I got up and threw away my apple core. "Janey knows what the bad things are that Sid does."

"She does? What do you know? It doesn't surprise me."

"She knows about sex?"

Mae frowned. "I'm not sure if she knows what exactly it is, but she knows it involves men and women, and that you're supposed to be married." Mae shrugged. "I wouldn't worry about it. If it were Darby or Ellen, maybe. But Janey seems to be beyond corruption. I don't think she tells me half what she sees and you wouldn't believe what she does tell me she knows, even about you."

"What's she said?" I gasped, terrified that Janey was onto Sid's and my business.

Mae laughed. "Nothing bad. Just little things, like how you and Sid feel about each other."

"We're just friends. Very close friends, but that's it."

"Right." With a knowing grin, Mae shook her head. "Don't worry about Janey, Lisa. I've spent a lot of time talking with her and she's got her head on straighter about moral issues than I do."

"I guess." Morosely, I opened the refrigerator door again.

"Lisa, I do want to talk to you."

My heart froze, wondering if Janey had put Mae onto the business after all. My eyes were past seeing what there was to eat, but I kept my nose in the refrigerator anyway.

"What about?" I asked as casually as I could.

"I'm just concerned, that's all. Lisa, you've never been that open and it seems like lately you've been even more withdrawn. I can't help wondering if there's something you're hiding."

Oh, there wasn't much, just the fact that I'm a counter-espionage agent, risking my neck on a regular basis for the safety of the free world as we know it. But I'm not allowed to mention that little fact, even to my family, and even if I were, I'm not sure I would. I grabbed at the more obvious conclusion.

"You mean like Sid and me?" I grabbed a tub of yogurt and all but slammed the refrigerator door shut.

Mae sank into a chair at the table. "Lisa, please don't get mad at me, but-"

"But nothing!" I slammed the silverware drawer open and grabbed a spoon. "This is incredible. Even my own sister doesn't trust me. Mae, you know me better than that."

"That's just the point. I don't know you. You don't let me. You don't let anybody know you. Good lord, look how long it took you just to tell me you were living at Sid's house."

"I just didn't get around to it." Leaning against the counter, I opened the yogurt and licked the lid. "And you're the one who doesn't want me telling Mama and Daddy."

"I'm supposed to be the bad guy because I don't want a fist fight to break out on a holiday?"

"If Daddy was going to get violent with Sid, he would have this week. Trust me, he's had ample provocation. Both of them have, and nothing's come of it."

"Really? Daddy's ribs are in bad shape again, and Sid has one heck of a shiner."

I rolled my eyes. "That was Donny Severn and his gang. Sid and Daddy had patched things up, more or less. Daddy even said Sid had one hell of a punch."

"That's pretty good for Daddy. But what about you, Lisa?"

"What about me?"

"Why can't you talk to me?"

I looked away. "I just can't. And don't ask why because that's all the answer you're going to get."

Sid came in. "I should have known to look for you in here. Oh. Hi, Mae."

Mae sighed. "Hi, Sid."

"Well." Sid looked at the two of us, trying to figure out what was going on. He took a deep breath and changed the subject. "It appears the children want to have lunch in the main lodge and your mother is insisting we indulge them. So, Lisa, you and I have to hurry and change into more casual clothes."

"Sure." I finished off my yogurt and dumped the tub in the trash and the spoon in the sink, then followed Sid out.

He stopped me in front of his room. "I don't really want to bring up a sore spot, but I do want to apologize for laughing at your prom picture."

"It's wasn't that big a deal," I snorted.

"It wouldn't have been, but for your date's preference, and that little hassle you had last month."

I'd gone out a couple times with a guy who turned out to be gay and was only going out with me because he was still in the closet and needed a woman around to look good. Rick felt pretty bad about misleading me, but I have to admit it had hurt. Somehow, in spite of it, we were getting to be friends.

I shrugged. "Well, now you know how it happened."

"I wish I'd known before." Sid gazed at me thoughtfully. "After you left, Mae started complained about how withdrawn you are and how you never tell anyone anything."

"I tell you stuff."

"Not everything."

"I guess not." I sighed. "I just don't tell people things. The funny part is, I've told you more than I've ever told anyone, even Leslie Bowan." I looked at him with a small smile. "I guess you and I have more in common than we thought."

Sid chuckled. "I suppose I shall have to learn how to pull answers out of you like you do to me."

"I'm sorry." I blushed.

"No. I'm glad you do. It's made all the difference. We'd better get going." He looked over at the door to the bedroom and frowned. "I thought I left this closed."

It was open just a crack, about an inch or two at the most. Cautiously, Sid pushed it open the rest of the way, then swore a blue streak.

His suitcase lay open in the middle of the floor and his clothes were strewn all over the place. My first thought was that some enemy had searched it, but there was another more likely source.

"Those twins," I groaned. "They were supposed to stay in the kitchen. I should have known something was up when they weren't there. I'm sorry, Sid."

"It's not your fault." Disgusted, Sid started picking up. "If anything, I did it to myself. I should have locked the case and put it out of their reach."

I picked up a shirt. "There's no such thing. They've gotten stuff out of the top of Mae's closet. Is anything missing?"

Sid went through the case, then again, and swore softly. He went through the case a third time, checking every pocket, then turning the case upside down.

"What's gone?" I asked.

He got up and checked outside the room. "That second package of cocaine we found. I brought it in to verify it with my test kit and hid it in my suitcase, and it is coke, and only cut once."

"Oh, my god." I crossed myself. "You think Marty and Mitch got it?"

"Who else could have?" Sid searched the room, getting on his knees and looking under the bed. "Unless it's in this room somewhere, they've got it. They wouldn't try eating it, would they?"

I went through the closet. "I don't think so. They're very good about not putting stuff in their mouths. Sid, how are we going to ask them?"

"We're going to have to somehow, and do it very carefully, or we could blow our whole cover."

We combed the room. No little box or white powder. There was a knock on the door.

"Hey, you two," Neil called from the other side.

"By any lucky chance are you fooling around in there?"

"For crying out loud!" I stomped over to the door and whipped it open. "Neil, I have had it. There is nothing going on between Sid and me. He is not my boyfriend. We are not sleeping together. There is nothing, repeat nothing, romantically oriented going on between us!"

"Okay," Neil replied, completely unperturbed.

I swallowed my anger down somewhat. "I am amazed that Mae did not bash your head in years ago."

Neil shrugged. "Mom wants to know what's taking so long."

"Your sons, Martin and Mitchell." I stepped back so he could see the mess. "They got into Sid's stuff and threw it all over."

"Oh." Neil shook his head. "I'm sorry, Sid. Can I help you get it back together?"

"No thanks, Neil," said Sid. "I've more or less got it under control."

"Okay. I'll take care of the twins. But you guys hurry. We're all waiting on you." Neil ambled off, presumably in search of his errant sons.

"What now?" I asked Sid when we were alone again.

"We change clothes and go to lunch." Sid put his hand on my shoulder. "We can't ask them outright with the adults around just in case they didn't find it. If they don't put stuff in their mouths, it should be okay."

The twins were doing time out in the living room when we joined the others. We had to wait another three minutes for them, and then more minutes while they tearfully apologized to Sid. I watched them nervously. There weren't any signs of the box, or worse, its contents on them, and they weren't acting sick. I had a feeling if they'd eaten cocaine, something would have been happening by then. [They'd have been dead - SEH]

Mae and Neil didn't say anything, and I know they would have if they'd found the box. Altogether, it was a very tense lunch, even if Sid and I didn't let on that we were tense about anything. After lunch, I brought Motley into Sid's room, but he didn't find anything. I was going to take him around the house, but Sid stopped me, saying it would look too suspicious, and that we'd do it that night after everyone was asleep.

The afternoon dragged. Sid chatted comfortably, but I couldn't. I never was any good at small talk. I did try to forget about the cocaine. The kids were fine and not acting funny, so I didn't think they had it. I can usually tell when they're hiding something. So I figured Marty and Mitch must have dropped the box somewhere. That relaxed me some, but it didn't help the clock move any faster.

Just after dinner, the doorbell rang. Mama got it and was not happy. Sheriff's Investigator Carl Lehrer had managed to convince a California judge that he had probable cause for a search warrant on Sid and me. He had with him from the South Lake Tahoe P.D. a detective named Frisch, two uniform officers, and a policewoman to pat me down.

Mae got a good grip on Murbles and Richmond, but they were pretty mellow. Motley growled low and mean at Lehrer, but I had a good grip him.

"And just what are you looking for, Carl Lehrer?" snarled Daddy.

Lehrer puffed himself up. "I have very good reason to believe that these two are hiding a missing drug shipment that was supposed to come to Murray Waters. This is the second time drugs have turned up missing and these two have been involved."

I handed Motley to Neil, then rolled my eyes as the policewoman patted me down.

"She's clean," she said.

"That is the most ridiculous thing I have heard in my life," snapped Daddy.

Mama glared. "Who do you think you are, Carl Lehrer? The Gestapo?"

Lehrer waived the warrant. "The court doesn't

think so. Where are these two staying?"

Mama showed him and the other officers back. The kids came running out and clung to their parents.

"Why are they picking on Sid and Lisa?" Mae asked, irritated. "As if either of them would have drugs on them."

I glanced at Sid. His eyes briefly caught mine. Apparently, Mae hadn't found the box. Sid and I were wondering if Lehrer would.

Some minutes later, he returned to the living room with my purse in his hands and Frisch on his tail.

"I know what I'm doing," Lehrer was saying. He went over to the coffee table and emptied my purse onto it. "Well, look at this." He picked up the roll of strapping tape and brought it over to me. "Tape." He shoved the roll in my face. "You know what this is used for."

It's used by undercover espionage agents to bind prisoners because carrying handcuffs looks funny. It took every ounce of self-control that I had to contort my face into a puzzled frown, instead of letting out the panic I felt.

"Mailing packages?" I asked.

Lehrer looked over at Sid, who shrugged.

"Lehrer, what the hell are you doing?" asked Frisch, who had been completely disgusted with the whole venture from the start. "Just because she has tape doesn't mean she used it to ship coke." He went through the stuff on the coffee table. "So she keeps the kitchen sink in her purse. That's not illegal, and I don't see anything here that is."

Snarling, Lehrer dropped the roll on the coffee table and went to check on the other officers. Frisch sighed and shook his head.

"I'm sorry about this, Bill," he said to my father.

Daddy shrugged.

"Well, damn it, it's got to be around here someplace," Lehrer yelled from the back. "I know they have it." He eventually stomped back into the living room, followed by the other three officers. "Alright, damn it, you're clean." He stomped over to Sid and me. "I don't know how you did it, but you're clean. But I know it's around here someplace, and I am going to watch you two like a hawk until I find it. Get that?"

"Lehrer, you're overstepping your bounds," said Frisch. "You didn't find anything. Let's get out of here."

Daddy showed the officers out and stayed outside. As they left, I gathered together the stuff from my purse, surreptitiously switching on my bug finder. The flash was weak, but definitely there.

"What kind of trouble are you two in?" Mae asked, letting the two big dogs go. They joined Motley in barking at the front door.

"I don't want to talk about it," I said, sweeping my pens, a hair pick, and several dirty Lifesavers into my purse. "I'm going to my room."

The flash on the bug finder grew bright and steady as I went in. Motley pushed in past me and started sniffing. Before I could get the bug finder to zero in, he'd found the bug. It was stuck under my bookshelf. I took Motley into Sid's room just to be on the safe side. Motley found the bug under a bookshelf in there. I left quickly to find Sid.

He was right outside the door.

"I thought you might be upset," he said.

"I guess," I said out loud, then mouthed the word "wired" and pointed to his room.

Sid pointed at my room. "Look, it's his problem."

"Wired," I mouthed, then said aloud, "I know."

"This is the second time he has searched us and found nothing. There is never going to be anything for him to find, so sooner or later he is going to completely lose credibility, assuming he hasn't already."

"You're right."

"Come on. Let's go relax on the porch."

I brought the bug finder with me. It was chilly out on the back porch, which meant the windows were closed, and the bedrooms are on the side of the house, so there was no one to hear us. I checked anyway.

"Nothing transmitting," I muttered. "But what about those mikes that pick up everything from five hundred feet away?"

Sid laughed. "They have a very limited usefulness precisely because they can pick up everything. It's much too noisy here with all those cabins with people in them." He looked over at me. "We've been bugged."

"And he knows what tape is for."

Sid nodded. "That does not speak well of him. But it is possible he is on our side."

"That is not a comforting thought."

"Not in the least. But until we know where the secrets are, we can't say for sure he's a bad guy. I just wish I knew where the cocaine is. It must be out on the grounds somewhere."

The door behind us opened and the screen door creaked. Given what Janey had for us, you could say she was right on cue.

"Uncle Sid, Aunt Lisa," she said nervously. "I think I know what those policemen were looking for." She pulled the remains of a small cardboard box from her sweatshirt pocket.

Jolted, Sid and I looked at each other.

"Where did you get this?" I asked, taking it from her.

"The twins were tearing it apart this morning," Janey said. "There was a white powder in it."

"Where is the powder?" Sid asked.

Janey shrugged and pointed. "All over the place, but mostly over by those trees next to the parking lot." She looked over at Sid, her big eyes full of fear. "Is it yours, Uncle Sid?"

"No," he said softly and pulled her into his lap. "Your aunt and I found it, and we kept it because we were trying to find who brought it here. We just didn't want the police to find it because we knew Investigator Lehrer would not believe us when we told him it wasn't ours."

"He's a very bad man," said Janey. She sighed. "I guess I shouldn't say that."

"Why not, Janey?" I asked.

"My teacher at school, Mrs. Fenner? I told her that Bobby Drexel was bad, 'cause I figured if Mrs. Fenner and I were really nice to him, he'd stop being bad. Only she got really mad at me." Janey sighed. "Bobby doesn't do anything bad, but I can tell he is, and I wanted him to be okay. Mrs. Fenner didn't understand."

I sighed. "I know that feeling."

Morose, I played with the shred of cardboard. It was the longer, wider side of the box, with the end flap still attached and covered with packing tape.

"It's alright," said Janey. "I like talking with you, Aunt Lisa. You understand."

I smiled. "I do my best."

She kissed Sid's cheek, then scrambled free. "I'm going to bed now."

"Uh, Janey," said Sid cautiously. "I'm not big on secrets, but I think it would be better if we kept that little box business just between us."

"I know." Janey opened the screen door. "I wasn't going to tell."

The kitchen door slammed behind her.

"She knows a lot more than she talks about," I said, picking at the tape on the box.

"Just like someone else I know." Sid grinned at me.

"She could very easily be onto our business."

"To be honest, I've been wondering if she is. However, in the first place, I doubt she'll say anything, and in the second, there's not a damned thing we can do about it if she is."

I lifted the tape from the end flap. Something funny flashed in the porch light.

"What?" I muttered.

"You find something?" Sid leaned over.

"You're blocking the light." I wriggled around. "It's a piece of film." I pulled it out. "A microdot."

Sid took it. "Great, and your viewer's inside."

"I'll go get it." I was inside in a flash.

I got the viewer from my purse without fussing about the bug. Lehrer would have no way of knowing what I'd gone in there for. I got back out to the porch without getting stopped by the rest of my family.

Sid put the dot in the viewer while I watched the door.

"I'll be damned," he muttered.

"Why don't I get to see," I complained. "I found it."

Sid handed me the viewer. It was filled with schematics. I turned it off.

"Why smuggle secrets in with drugs?" I asked.

"Just hazarding a guess, who's going to look for them once the drugs are found?" Sid sat back down on the steps. "And keep in mind, smuggling secrets will get you in a lot more trouble than smuggling drugs will. You get caught smuggling cocaine and you've got a whole cartel behind you with suitcases of cash for bail money. Get caught with secrets and nobody's going to acknowledge you, not even the government you're spying for. You're on your own."

"Does Lehrer know about this?"

Sid shrugged. "He's pretty anxious to get a hold of the shipment. We're mostly sure he's dealing coke. It's not unlikely he was behind Della's death. I'd say there's pretty good odds he's our mole. The trick now will be proving it."

"Maybe we ought to try a break in tonight while he's on duty."

Sid shook his head. "Not while we're wired. We can't leave until after everyone else is in bed, and after that, Lehrer will hear us and wonder."

"Or won't hear you and wonder."

"What do you mean?"

I chuckled. "You talk in your sleep, remember?"

"Oh. That."

"Don't you ever worry about revealing secrets?"

"I have yet to." Sid gazed up at the sky. "At least,

I have reason to believe I haven't. I suspect it's because even my subconscious knows I can't, nor do I want to. It's sort of like hypnosis, in that even in a trance you're not going to do anything you really don't want to do."

"Like if I got hypnotized, I wouldn't strip and run naked."

Sid got up and stretched. "Look at all those stars." [And yes, I was deliberately changing the subject. I was having too much fun imagining you hypnotized and open to suggestion - SEH]

"You poor, deprived urbanite." I smiled. "There are only two things I really miss when I'm not in the mountains, clean air and stars at night."

"Them's the breaks. Come on. We'd better get back inside before I find myself explaining things to your father."

"There's nothing to explain."

Sid's hot little smile made me catch my breath.

"'Tis a pity," he said softly.

September 23, 1983

Friday morning, Sid decided he wanted a change of pace, so we ran up the road towards town, instead of south towards Meyers. Motley tagged along as usual.

"The hard part will be dismantling those bugs," said Sid. "We'll have to do that before anything else. The problem is that Lehrer is wondering about us."

"Why?" I grumbled, still not awake.

"I would imagine the missing coke. He's got a point about that, and there was the tape in your purse."

"It's not that strange a thing to carry."

"But you'd question someone who had it, wouldn't you?"

I just yawned. Sid sighed.

"What's the matter?" I asked.

"Nothing much," he said forlornly. "Just the usual. Last night, when you mentioned the possibly of your stripping and running naked, I naturally began thinking about it, and remembered that Tuesday was the last time I got any."

"So go out tonight."

Sid winced. "It'll be a little awkward with your family around. I was thinking I could make it through the weekend, but..."

His voice trailed off as his gaze settled on a young woman jogging towards us on the other side of the road. She wasn't wearing a bra. Sid's eyes weren't exactly going up and down, but you could tell what they were focused on.

"She's doing horrible things to her chest," I said.

Sid wrenched his eyes away. "I keep thinking what I'd like to be doing to it."

"We could run to the lake and I could dump you in."

"No thanks. I think I'll just run some errands by myself this morning."

"How are you going to do that at this time of day without buying it?"

Sid sighed. "That could be somewhat problematic. But don't worry. I will not be patronizing any brothels or hookers."

I shook my head. I didn't doubt it.

We had just turned around when two more women, both rather plump and wearing pastel running suits turned the corner and jogged towards us.

"Oh my," gasped one. "Sarah, look. It's Lisa Wycherly. Hi, Lisa!"

I smiled, but inside I groaned. I wasn't quite sure who they were, the two having gained some since high school. Sarah had to be Sarah Jefferson, and her partner looked a lot like Rhonda Stadtler. I wasn't too thrilled to see either of them.

The girls I went to high school with tended to run to extremes. Either they went all the way with their boyfriends or they believed that you didn't kiss a boy until you were engaged to him. Rhonda and Sarah were from the latter extreme. In fact, their big hobby had been planning different ways to avoid sleeping in the same bed as their husbands on their wedding nights. I noticed they both wore wedding bands.

It would have been rude not to stop, and I have to admit I didn't mind that part of it.

"Hello, Lisa, it's so good to see you," crowed Sarah.

Rhonda was giving Sid the once over. Actually, so was Sarah, but there was something different about the way Rhonda ogled. She was almost hungry.

"Hi, you guys," I said. "It's nice to see you. Um, this is my boss, Sid. I'm sorry, I don't know your married names."

Rhonda smiled at Sid. "I'm Rhonda Jefferson, and this is Sarah Carter."

"Nice to meet you," said Sid, his gaze lingering on Rhonda.

Sarah didn't notice. "You haven't changed a bit, Lisa, except for that perm. It looks great. I wish I could say the same." She giggled. "I put on so much weight with my last baby."

Apparently, she'd resigned herself to sleeping with her husband somewhere along the line.

"How many do you have?" I asked politely.

"Five." She giggled proudly.

"When did you get married?" I gasped.

"August after we graduated. You knew I was engaged to Fred Carter, didn't you?"

"Oh, that's right." It had been the ideal engagement for Sarah. Fred had been in the army the whole time, and they had courted each other through the mail. "Is Fred out of the army?"

"Oh, yeah. We bought his parents motel, and Fred's talking about expanding."

"How nice."

"You look like you're doing really well."

"Pretty good."

Sarah giggled again. "I've heard all the rumors. Lynn Fremont, you know, she used to be Lynn Raines, met me in the supermarket the other day. Her husband works at that hotel, so she heard everything first hand. She said she couldn't believe that you, of all people, would be involved like that."

I sighed. Lynn was from the other extreme and had always put me down because I wasn't.

I smiled weakly. "I guess I still get the last laugh. There's nothing going on."

Sarah glanced over at Sid, who was talking quietly with Rhonda.

"There isn't?" She giggled.

"There isn't." The frost crept into my voice.

Motley whined.

"We'd better get going," said Sid suddenly.

We said good-bye and resumed our run.

"What were you and Rhonda talking about?"

Sid chuckled. "I don't think you want to know."

"You don't mean you and her..?"

"It was her idea, and it is pretty convenient."

"You're kidding. I mean, I saw her looking at you, but it just doesn't make sense. Rhonda's always been one of the most uptight prudes I've ever met."

"She's changed a lot since you knew her."

"She's married."

"So she said, to Sarah's brother, as a matter of fact."

"Doesn't that bother you?"

"That she's married?" Sid shrugged. "You know I believe marriage is a lie, and if she agrees, why should it bother me?

"What about her husband?"

"According to Rhonda, he doesn't care, and there was just enough bitterness in her tone to tell me he doesn't. If my guess is right, he's probably running around himself."

"Possibly because he can't get it at home."

Sid laughed. "I stand warned. But I'm not worried."

"Well, I hope he doesn't catch you. You've already got one black eye."

"That's why I usually avoid married women. Violence is so messy."

I glanced at Sid, suddenly very glad he had no interest in marriage. I could see the two of us trapped in a loveless union, taking lovers to get back at each other. Or I tried to see us that way. Somehow, I just couldn't. [Probably because neither of us really wanted to be married at that point. The cold, hard truth about Rhonda was that she was raised to look to men for validation, and married the first man she could find to get away from her parents. Pete Jefferson had been fooling around on her almost from the start. Rhonda got into it shortly after when one of the managers at the store where she worked seduced her. It was technically sexual harassment, but he ended up making her feel so good, she kept it up and found other lovers, too - SEH]

When we got back to the house, Sid went straight

for the shower. The kids were up and dressed and playing outside with Richmond and Murbles. Motley and I played with them for a while, then I wandered into the kitchen. Mama and Mae were also up and dressed and cutting up fruit for breakfast.

"Oh, you're back," said Mama. "How you doing this morning?"

"Fine." I went over and kissed her cheek. "How are you?"

"Real good, honey," she replied without her usual enthusiasm.

"And how are you, sister the elder?" I hugged Mae from behind. "Sleep okay?"

Mae yawned. "Uh-huh."

I grabbed a chunk of cantaloupe and popped it in my mouth.

"Lisa Jane," scolded Mama. "You keep your hands out of that bowl."

"Yes, Mama." I grabbed the last banana and peeled it part way down. Taking a bite, I flopped into a chair.

"Why don't you get a knife and help us?" Mama asked.

"I've been helping all week. It's Mae's turn."

"Young lady, that is so childish. Landsakes. Mae works hard all the time, feeding all those kids. You just have yourself to feed."

"Which is a monumental task in itself," said Sid, grinning. He'd come in while Mama was talking, wearing a suit and tie.

"All dressed up again, Sid?" Mama said with a disappointed sigh.

"I'm afraid I've got some business to attend to. I just came in to tell Lisa I'm through in the bathroom."

"Well, you're not leaving on an empty stomach. Here." Mama dished fruit into a bowl. "I've got toast in the oven. I'll get it."

"Thanks." Sid found the last spot at the table.

"Lisle, why don't you hurry and get dressed so you don't hold up Sid," said Mama, laying a placemat in front of Sid.

"She's not coming with me." Sid spread his napkin on his lap while Mama put a plate of toast next to the bowl of fruit.

"She's not?"

"Nope." I finished my banana.

Mae snickered at Sid. "What are you up to?"

Sid grinned. "I'll never tell."

"Now you two stop it," scolded Mama. "'Tisn't nice to talk like that. What if one of the kids heard you?"

"Mama, are you sure you're okay?" I asked. "You seem a little snippy this morning."

Mama glared. "Just never you mind about me. I'm fine." She looked out the window, then strode over to the back door. "Darby! I told you to stay out of that wood pile."

The screen door creaked and slammed as she went out, hollering at the kids.

"It's the cops," sighed Mae. "Daddy talked to Detective Frisch for a long time last night after that Lehrer guy left. I guess South Lake Tahoe P.D. didn't know anything about any drugs connected to Murray's death until Lehrer showed up with the warrant, so Daddy called Douglas County Sheriff's this morning. They don't know anything about any drug shipments, either. I overheard Mama hollering at Daddy about sticking his nose in where it doesn't belong, and that he should let the DEA handle it."

"They're involved?" I asked casually, avoiding Sid's eyes. "What's going on?"

Mae shrugged. "I don't know. Mama won't say."

The screen door creaked and slammed.

"Well, that's enough of that," grumbled Mama.

"Althea, I'm inclined to agree," said Sid, wiping his mouth. "And so I really must be off."

"Are you sure can't take care of your business here?" Mama asked as Sid got up.

"I'm very sure." Sid brought his dishes over to the sink.

"Well, Sid, you're perfectly welcome to bring a guest here, if you like."

"Mama, why don't you just let him go?" I said quickly before Sid could reply.

"I'll be back by lunch." Sid grinned and left.

"He's sure starting early," Mae whispered to me.

"He figures it'll be too awkward to go out tonight," I whispered back.

"But how's he going to pick up somebody at this hour of the day?"

"He's got it all arranged." I sighed. "I'm glad he's going, frankly. He's a terrible grouch when he gets horny, and it's been a while."

Mae snickered. "That's not what I've been hearing."

"He hasn't been out since Tuesday, and for him, that's a while."

Mae giggled.

"What are you two whispering about?"

"Nothing, Mama," said Mae. "'Tisn't nice."

"Well, I'm going to get dressed," I announced, grabbing another piece of cantaloupe and getting a piece of toast from the oven. "Save me some breakfast, will you?"

I showered and changed in record time into jeans and a shirt. I pulled my Shetland wool sweater on as I headed for the kitchen. I paused outside the door, pulling my collar out.

"I know what you mean about them," Mama was saying on the other side.

"But you're not going to get them to admit it," said Mae. "Even to themselves."

"Well, the way things stand right now, I think it's just as well."

[Were they talking about us, by any chance? - SEH]

I pushed open the door. "What's just as well?"

They both colored up and looked at each other with guilty starts.

"Nothing," said Mae, too quickly.

[I guess they were. It's interesting how they picked up on our feelings for each other so early. Too bad we hadn't - SEH]

I was puzzled but decided not to pursue it.

"Where's the food?" I asked instead.

"I'm sorry, Lisle," groaned Mama. "They went and ate up everything before I could save you some."

"You probably wouldn't have saved enough anyway." I grinned. "Besides, I happen to know there's something in the cupboard that I like and now that the boss is safely occupied elsewhere..."

I all but danced to the cupboard and opened it.

Mae groaned. "Lisa, I hope that's not what I think that is."

"Oh, yes it is, Mae." I hugged the fuschia colored box. "Lucky Charms in all its sugar-coated glory. Fortified with artificial preservatives and colors."

I grabbed a medium-sized mixing bowl out of the other cupboard, a soup spoon, and the milk. I put the bowl at my spot at the table and emptied the box into the bowl.

"Are you going to eat all that?" asked Mae, utterly disgusted.

"You bet I am." I picked a coupon and a plastic wrapped toy out of the cereal and poured on the milk. "And I am going to enjoy every bite, without lectures on what it's doing to my insides. You wouldn't believe what a time Mama and I had getting this past Sid. Frankly, Mama, I think Sid went to the grocery store with us just to keep an eye on me. He's such a control freak."

"He's just looking out for your own well-being," said Mae.

"Mae, shut up." I shoveled it in.

"Lisa Jane, you don't talk to your sister like that," said Mama. "She's just concerned."

"I know. But there's nothing to be concerned about. Really." I went back to my cereal.

I didn't see it, but I could tell Mama and Mae were

shaking their heads. There wasn't anything I could do about it, so I went on eating my cereal.

When I finished, I washed my bowl and put it away and wandered back towards my room. I was in the front entry when the phone rang. Mama got it, then hollered for Daddy.

"In the living room," he hollered back.

"It's that DEA guy again," called Mama.

"I'll take it in the bedroom."

My parents' bedroom is right next to mine, and mine was bugged. I beat it out of the hall and to my room, where I turned on the radio and tuned it to a rock and roll station. Then I slid into the hallway to the closed door to my parents' bedroom. I had no idea why Daddy was talking to someone from the Drug Enforcement Agency, but I was going to find out.

"Aunt Lisa!" Janey hissed. She tugged on my arm. "This way."

"But-"

I glanced at the door, then took a chance and followed her back to the hall phone. Mama and Mae had the extension off the hook and their ears pressed to the receiver. Mama quickly put a finger to her lips. I shoved my way in, dislodging Mae, who glared at me furiously. I didn't care. She didn't have priority need to know, and I did, even if I couldn't tell her that.

"Douglas County said they didn't know squat about it," said Daddy's voice. "It just seems kind of fishy to me, and Lehrer was awful anxious about finding it."

"You think he knows something?" asked the DEA guy. His voice sounded familiar but I couldn't place it.

Mae squeezed in. I held my ground and put my finger in my free ear.

"He'd almost have to," said Daddy. "Neither of us said a word about the stuff from the store, even with Murray dead, and Lehrer was very clear. There were two missing shipments."

"If we could just figure out where the one Riordan had went to."

"Lehrer sure as hell doesn't know, and he wants to, bad."

"And he's looking for a second shipment. The question is, did it come in before or after Murray died?"

"Well, the police say he died Friday night."

"Hm." The DEA guy thought for a moment. "Do you know if you got anything from Sunland on Friday?"

"I don't think so. But they ain't sending it through the stock. We got the winter order in this past Tuesday and there wasn't anything there that shouldn't have been, or anything missing, either."

"Who unpacked it?"

"My daughter and that boss of hers. She would have said something if she found it."

"I agree, but there's her boss. He was humping Riordan when the stuff she had disappeared."

"I don't think he's messing with drugs. He's too busy chasing tail."

"I've heard he's got money. You know where it comes from?"

"Well now, they've never said." Daddy mused. "Nah. Lisa's been with him for a year. She'd have noticed by now if he was up to something funny."

"What if he's got some kind of hold on her. Is she scared of him at all?"

Daddy snorted. "I sure wish she were. Look, the stuff's got to be coming in through some kind of courier. We've been over and over that stock thing, and there's no way Murray could have kept finding it faster than we could, not without radar."

[Or a good dog - SEH]

"All I know is that Riordan told me she was to deliver a back order to the store. It's possible it was a code to someone else in the store, maybe that Martin kid."

"I'm inclined to think not. I think she knows something about what's going on, but she just ain't that bright."

"Well, Bill, I don't know what to tell you. I guess

we'll have to try checking out Lehrer. Tell you what. He's on duty tonight. We'll go over to his place after he's on and check it out."

"Ain't that illegal?"

"There's ways around it. That's why I need you there."

Daddy cleared his throat. "If I'm under oath, I'm going to say what really happened."

The DEA guy laughed. "I just need you to set Lehrer up. It's not going to blow the court case, and you probably won't have to testify, let alone perjure yourself. Even then, chances are, we'll get him to name names, and plea bargain it. Let's see. Lehrer's night shift. I think those guys have roll call at eleven. Why don't you meet me at the store at eleven thirty and we'll go over from there."

"Eleven thirty, alright. I'll meet you in the back."

"Hey, with luck, Lehrer'll be able to tell us who killed Murray, and maybe even Riordan. Talk to you later."

They hung up. Mama all but slammed the phone down and pressed her lips together.

"I don't like it," she hissed, hurrying into the kitchen. "I just don't like it."

"What's Daddy been doing with the DEA?" I demanded, right on her heels.

"And what did you think you were doing pushing me out?" snapped Mae, grabbing my shoulder and spinning me around.

"I needed to hear," I said.

"I was there first."

"Well, nobody's trying to pin a bum drug rap on you."

"Everyone knows that's just hot air. You were just being selfish again."

"Girls!" snapped Mama. "Landsakes, you're both grown women. It's about time you stopped bickering with each other."

"Mama, I was there first and she pushed me off,"

groaned Mae.

"What's Daddy doing with the DEA?" I pressed. "Come on, Mama. I need to know."

Mama sank down into a chair and leaned against the table with her head in her hand.

"Somebody's been smuggling drugs through your daddy's store," she said softly. "We don't know who. The only reason they think it's Murray is 'cause he got killed. The fellow from the DEA said it's through Sunland Products, and that's why it's Daddy's store. It's the closest place to the state line that carries sporting goods, and it carries Sunland year-round."

I sat down next to her. "How long has this been going on?"

"Don't know about the smuggling. Daddy and the guy from the DEA have been talking for about a month now." Mama shook her head. "I'm just so afraid he's going to get his neck in too deep."

So was I, knowing that espionage was involved, too.

"Oh, Mama," said Mae, sitting down on her other side. "Daddy's not stupid, and he knows how to handle himself. He'll be fine."

Daddy walked in. "Lisle, what are you doing in here? I thought you were in your room. And why are you playing that damn radio so loud?"

"I just had it on." I shrugged with a guilty smile. "And then, well..."

Daddy's eyes narrowed. "You girls were listening in. Don't think I didn't know."

"Well, Bill, I think we needed to." Mama got up, spitting mad. "With that DEA guy and his midnight meetings. You're going to get yourself killed if you're not careful. These drug dealers don't play nice. Landsakes, you read in the papers every darned day about one of them fellows getting themselves murdered, or what have you."

"I know what I'm doing, Althea."

"Oh, you do. Since when did you join the DEA?"

"If the man needs help and I can do it, it's the least I can do. He won't let me do anything dangerous anyway." Daddy sighed and held Mama. "Honey, I'm going to be careful and stay out of the way. I know my limitations."

"Oh, Bill, I just don't want to see you hurt." She looked up at him. "I know you can handle yourself, but you be careful now."

Daddy gave her a squeeze and released her. "Well, it's getting on for time. Where's Neil? We need to fire up the barbecue."

There were steaks and chicken, grilled, and Mama's special potato salad and green salad, and potatoes roasted in the coals, and vegetable kebobs. The only thing missing was the corn on the cob, but it was too late in the year for that. Sid showed up just in time to change into jeans and sweater and eat. I did manage to signal him that we needed to talk as soon as possible and slipped off into the woods the minute I was done eating. Sid found me in a nearby clearing some minutes later.

"Well?" he asked.

I told him about the phone call. He was, as I expected, thrilled.

"Jesus," he swore.

"Sid!"

He rolled his eyes. "I'm sorry. But this is one complication we can't afford."

"No kidding." I picked up a twig and started peeling its bark off.

"We'll have to work around it. The first priority will be to dismantle those bugs."

"There's always the radio. I think mine is still on."

"Someone's bound to turn it off at just the wrong moment." He shook his head. "We'll find a way. We just have to think about it. I did get a good look at the one in my room last night. It's more Company equipment."

"It is?" I frowned. "At least, we know who got the stolen equipment."

Sid nodded.

"Now what?" I asked.

"Another excellent question."

"So we're stuck."

"For the moment." He smiled at me. "I hear you've got sugar on your breath."

"Mae ratted on me, didn't she?" I viciously tossed away a piece of bark.

"Yes."

"Well, I don't want to hear any more about it. For once, will you just leave me alone?"

"What's the matter, Lisa?" His gentle eyes gazed at me.

"It's my dad." Trying not to cry, I turned away. "He doesn't know what he's getting into, with the spy stuff and all. And I can't tell him. And I couldn't tell Mae why I had to hog the phone this morning. And she's been on my case about being withdrawn. She's really worried about it. Okay, I never was that open, but I could at least say things if I wanted to. Now, it's like there's a barrier between me and my family and it hurts. You know, I really like this business most of the time. But there are days when I wonder if it's worth the sacrifices."

"Sometimes I wonder, too."

"Yeah, but it's easier for you, Sid. You don't have a family. You keep telling me you prefer being a loner."

"True. But I have my moments. Frankly, Lisa, I envy you. If something happens to you, there are people who will notice you've gone. Me, I'll fade away and no one will know the difference."

"Sid, that's not true."

He smiled. "Well, not anymore. I'm very grateful for your friendship, and for the way your sister's family adopted me. But in the circle of people I generally move in, one only exists for the moment you're there. And I don't want you feeling sorry for me. I like it that way. However, it has its drawbacks, just like having a family does. I do understand how you feel, Lisa. The business is a barrier, but a necessary one, and if you don't make the sacrifice, who will?"

"That's sort of what Father John keeps telling me. I'm in this situation because I can handle it better than anyone else. It just gets hard sometimes."

"Well, I'm here, and we have no excuse for a barrier."

I smiled softly. "No, we don't."

"By the way, I ran a couple errands while I was out."

"Either they were real quick ones, or Rhonda was."

Sid chuckled. "Somewhere in between." He sighed and shook his head. "Actually, she's involved in one sordid mess."

I went back to picking at my stick. "That's too bad."

"What is it about her that has you so bugged?"

"I wonder what could have happened to make her change so drastically, and I wonder if it could happen to me." I looked at him nervously. "It seems sometimes like I've got the perfect opportunity."

Sid smiled and shook his head. "If by that, you mean giving in to me, then no. Rhonda's problem has a lot more to do with an insensitive husband who made a promise he wasn't about to keep. I keep my promises, and I do my damnedest to be sensitive."

"And you're very successful. Still..."

"Lisa, it won't happen to you. You're much too strong. I can't think of anything that could happen to you that you couldn't rise above. You and Rhonda have very little in common that way."

"Thanks."

"Anyway, regarding those two errands. The first was a brief meeting with Tom Collins to see if he could confirm if our bugs were the stolen ones."

"And?"

"Assuming I described them accurately, they're pretty standard equipment."

"Oh, goody. A generic listening device."

Motley chose that moment to come trotting into

the clearing. He barked once, then whined softly as I bent to pet him. I suddenly smiled.

"Sid, why don't we let Motley find those bugs for us?"

"What do you mean?"

"Well, last night, when I was looking for them with the bug finder, Motley found them before I did. I pretended not to notice. But we could set it up to look like we finally did."

"Hm. That's a possible, but it might be a little tricky." He smiled down at Motley. "It would appear the mutt has his uses. Which brings me to my second errand. You may not have heard, but I found out that Murray's ex is in town with the children for the funeral tomorrow. Anyway, I sought her out, told her we had the dog, and she made it quite clear that the last thing she wanted was another dog around." He pulled a folded paper from his shirt pocket. "Anyway, here are Motley's papers. I do believe you have to sign and mail them in."

"Oh, Sid, thank you. How much do I owe you?"

"You don't."

"But-"

"I didn't have to pay for him. The former Mrs. Waters decided that between the hassle of paying for an ad and getting a vet to look at him, she was better off giving him away. It's hard enough to sell puppies. A year-old dog is almost impossible."

"But you don't want a dog."

"Don't you?"

"Yes, but I thought I was going to have to twist your arm or something."

He shrugged. "I thought I'd save you the trouble. He's all yours, Lisa. I've even called the fencing people to put in a kennel for him."

"Oh, Sid, that's wonderful. Thank you!"

I flung my arms around him and squeezed. He squeezed back.

"I'm so glad I've got you, Sid," I whispered.

"I'm so glad I've got you, Lisa."

We pulled apart. Gently, he laid his hand on my cheek. We gazed into each other's eyes for a minute, then softly, so softly, he laid a kiss on my lips.

Motley's barking brought us back down to earth. We could hear the children calling him, and he bounded off back to the house. Sid and I followed separately.

After lunch was cleaned up, the kids talked Sid into playing the piano for them. Darby had his guitar and played along, keeping up pretty well for someone who had only been playing since January.

"We're getting an orchestra together at school this year," he told Sid during a tuning break. "Only I won't get to be in it unless I learn to play something else. Mrs. Gomez says she already has a pianist and that she needs someone who's been playing a lot longer than I have. She thinks I ought to try violin."

Sid chuckled. "Boy, do I know how that feels. Almost the exact same thing happened to me when I started high school. Fortunately, my piano skills were already advanced by that point."

Darby shrugged. "I don't know. Violin sounds kind of neat, really. I just don't want to be called a sissy."

"That can be rough," said Sid. "But you know, the only real sissies are the ones who have to call others sissies."

Darby looked over at his grandfather. "What do you think, Grandpa?"

I knew why he asked. Darby and my father have kind of a strange relationship. Daddy was really ecstatic when he found he had a grandson. Even though I'd played substitute son for him, I was still his daughter, and after two of them, Daddy was looking forward to a real he-man to he-man relationship. Only Darby turned out to be anything but interested. Daddy was disappointed but equally determined that Darby should be what he is. Darby is onto him and makes a point of being a he-man whenever he can.

"Well, now..." Daddy struggled. "Darby, I've always

said you've got to follow your heart. If you want to play violin, then you play violin. Sid's right, and I think it takes a damned sight more guts to do something you want even though you might get called names than it does to do the name calling."

Darby didn't get a chance to answer. One of the twins started screaming from the back of the house.

"What now?" sighed Mae as the other twin joined in. Ellen wandered in. "Ellen, why are your brothers upset?"

She shrugged. "Janey's being mean to them. Motley found something neat in Uncle Sid's room and she took it away."

I glanced over at Sid.

He turned around on the piano bench. "What did they find, Ellen?"

She shrugged again. "Motley found another one in Aunt Lisa's room."

"Another what?" asked Mae.

Ellen shrugged. "It's neat."

"Janey!" called Neil. "Martin, Mitchell!"

"Daddy," bellowed Janey as she pushed her little brothers into the living room. "I told them to leave the things alone."

"What did they find, Janey?" asked Sid.

She held out her hand to display the two small round micro-transmitters. Neil picked them up.

"What the heck are these?" he asked. He looked at Janey. "Ellen said one was in Uncle Sid's room and the other was in Aunt Lisa's."

Janey nodded. "Yes."

Neil looked the bugs over closely. "I wonder if these are listening devices. Look at this wire mesh here."

"Are you sure one was in my room?" I said, letting my voice shake. Janey nodded. "Oh Lord, somebody's been listening to me?"

Neil started to show the bugs to Mae, but Daddy snatched them.

"If they are, I know who put them there," he

growled, looking the bugs over himself. "I've got a phone call to make."

"What if they're broadcasting, Daddy?" I asked, letting my voice go panicky.

Daddy stopped and looked at me. "You got a point."

"Is there an off switch?" I asked. I knew it was a dumb question, which is precisely why I asked.

"I wonder if I have that magnifying glass in the car," muttered Neil.

"Not the science kit," groaned Darby. Janey and Ellen looked at each other guiltily.

Neil's attempts to get the kids hooked on science are the family joke. The kids like science, especially Ellen. It's just that Neil thinks he is taking good advantage of serendipitous occasions, and the kids think he's a total bore. To be honest, Neil's lectures are a little on the dry side. [Dry doesn't begin to describe them. Sawdust has more flavor - SEH]

Neil sent Janey after the magnifying glass, which meant he knew darned well she and Ellen had hidden the science kit again. Meanwhile, I went to my room and checked my bug finder. Those adorable little brats had done their work well. Nothing was transmitting.

I went back to the living room. Neil had the eyeglass kit out, with the tiny screwdriver and pliers. Janey brought in the magnifying glass and everyone except the kids and me converged on the coffee table. Sid looked up and saw me standing in the doorway. Surreptitiously, I made a slicing motion across my neck. He nodded and slipped out of the pack.

We went back to his room.

"It's a pity we can't hire those kids to do our work for us more often," he said, shutting the door.

I stood next to it, listening for anyone coming.

"No kidding. Does this mean we go check out Lehrer tonight?"

"With your father and his friend from the DEA out to do the same? You'd better believe it. We'll just run a basic search and switch. I'll call Tom Collins and see if he can get us some less sensitive evidence."

"Maybe we ought to check out Donny Severn's place, too."

"Why? He couldn't have killed Murray. He was in Reno, remember?"

"Oh yeah." I felt deflated, then... "Sid, didn't Officer Burke say Stripkin said Donny was with him at the critical time?"

"That's why Donny's out of the running for Murray's murder."

"Except that Alice called Donny's friend Mike Friday night, and Mike said Donny wasn't there, that he was staying there but was out all the time."

Sid sat down on the bed and mused. "And that was before we said word one about Murray, which gives her even less reason to be lying about it." He looked at me. "Donny was supposedly in Reno since the previous Wednesday."

"Which was when Lehrer took Donny with him to do a job for him."

Sid snorted. "The problem is, with the gun that killed Della turning up the way it did, there's no way of proving that Donny did it."

"Unless that room service waiter identifies him."

Sid shook his head. "We have to get Donny arrested first. Actually, we need to get Lehrer arrested."

"Too bad we can't do it."

"Technically, we can." Sid got up and paced.

"A citizen's arrest, but anyone can do that."

"No. We have the authority to make a regular arrest for any crime under FBI jurisdiction. We just don't use it because it would blow our cover." He stopped pacing and gazed at the closet without seeing it. "Now, are you sure this DEA character plans to bust Lehrer tonight?"

"He said he needed Daddy to set Lehrer up, and the plan is to meet tonight."

An almost evil grin spread across Sid's face. "How about if we help the set up along?"

"How?"

"I still have Della's cocaine in the trunk of my car, and I seem to remember suggesting some drug charges might help things along."

"But don't we want him busted for espionage?"

"Yeah." Sid went back to pacing. "That would be preferable since they won't set him free quite as easily. But at the moment, I'll take any charges I can get. Did I give you the code nine phone number?"

"Yeah." Calling in a code nine brought out the nearest FBI agents who would make any arrests we needed made.

"Good. I'll put them on alert. With the DEA hanging around, it could get sticky if they butt heads. Now for the rest of the details."

It wasn't easy. We had to pull together all our equipment without anyone seeing us. We had to formulate a good excuse for being out that night without everyone else. I had to get Mama and Daddy to let me drive the jeep since Sid's car was a little too recognizable.

Sid got the stuff in from his car just as soon as it got dark, by hiding it under his ski jacket. It was also right on top of dinner, which is why there was no one around to see. I helped with the cleanup, then Mama sent me to get ready to go with Sid to a local nightclub that he was going to review for his article, which he also wanted my opinion on. Mae tagged along.

"Why aren't you staying here?" she asked softly. "You know Daddy has that meeting tonight."

"I know." I glanced at her bedroom, where Sid was checking over the guns and lockpicks and masks and gloves. "But, um, Sid didn't know anything about it when he set up the interview at the nightclub, and you know how Mama is. This past Wednesday, Sid told me to take off and she was really mad that I went riding instead of sticking around to help him. She doesn't need to worry about me losing my job on top of Daddy playing cops and robbers."

"I suppose. What are you going to wear?"

I squirmed. "Mae, I'd really rather get dressed by myself. Okay?"

Mae gave me the kind of look that said it wasn't but left me alone. I dressed quickly in a light pink handkerchief linen shirt I'd pressed and starched that afternoon, and my black break in pants. They were still pretty new, and the fabric hadn't faded yet, so they looked casual but nice. I also put on my armored running shoes. They were black, so I still looked a little dressed up. I pinned my hair up, then folded up the collar on my shirt to look stylish. I picked up a gray herringbone twill bomber jacket and with a deep breath, left the room.

I made sure the hall was empty and slid into Sid's room. He looked up from the bed where he was loading one of the S and W model thirteen three fifty-seven revolvers.

"You look good," he said.

He was wearing a white dress shirt, his shoulder holster and revolver, tight, dark jeans and his armored running shoes. A tweed sports jacket sat next to him on the bed.

"Thanks."

Sid rolled the clip, then clicked it in place and handed the gun and its holster to me. I slid it on. Sid slid into his sports coat.

"I'm almost tempted to put the model thirteen in my purse," I said, wriggling the holster around to where it was almost comfortable.

I pulled up the right leg of my pants and strapped on my twenty-two automatic.

Sid shrugged. "Anyplace you'll be carrying your purse, you won't be able to use it. You can't carry that monster with you on the break in, and I don't want to leave it out in an open car. We can't afford to lose it." He looked at me as I slid into my bomber jacket. "That's different. Where did you get it?"

"International Fabrics on Beverly." I zipped up the

front just high enough so I could get at the gun and still keep it hidden.

"It looks nice." Sid tried not to sigh.

He knows one of the reasons I sew most of my own clothes is because I'm basically cheap, which bothers him. It's not like he's underpaying me, and there's also my salary from Quickline. He can't understand why I won't spend one penny more than I have to. Neither can I, really. I've always been that way. [On the other hand, you do very good work, and I concede the therapeutic benefits are considerable - SEH]

I finished distributing lockpicks, miniature flashlights, glass cutters, wire cutters, screwdrivers, duct tape (a fresh roll I'd filched from the barn), and the box of cocaine among the many pockets in my pants.

"Are we ready?" Sid asked.

I took a deep breath. "Yeah."

We announced our departure and left quickly before anyone decided they wanted a hug. I'd seen to putting our ski jackets in the jeep earlier. I looked at Sid, then started the engine.

Not that we were really on our way yet. It was only eight o'clock, and we couldn't go near Lehrer's place until eleven. We did stop by a bar up the road in Stateline, just to back up what we'd told my family, and decided pretty quickly it didn't have anything to offer. We went back to the big casinos next to the state line, itself.

I made the pickup in the Keno Lounge. Tom Collins hid the microdots in a cocktail napkin which I slid into my pants. Then Sid and I hit the blackjack tables.

"I hope we have better luck tonight," he muttered as he busted again, and with twenty-two.

I crossed myself. I was doing okay, pretty much staying just a little bit ahead. I hit a blackjack the next hand.

By ten thirty, Sid was ahead fifty bucks, which wasn't much when you consider he'd been playing with twenty-five dollar chips. I was ahead twenty dollars, which was pretty darned good since I only bet the two dollar minimum. We cashed in and took off.

Lehrer's cabin was in Tahoe Village, off by itself at the end of a longish street. We drove by, then I parked the jeep in a real estate office's parking lot, behind some trees at the bottom of the hill. Sid and I slid out of our jackets and into our ski jackets and walked up the hill to Lehrer's place.

The cabin was dark, without even an outside light. In the trees next to the place, Sid and I put on our gloves and masks. We slipped onto the deck and over to the front door.

It was ajar. I glanced at Sid. He already had his revolver out. I drew mine. He backed up against the open side of the doorway. I backed up against the door side. We could hear nothing inside.

Sid nodded. I pushed the door open a little further. Sid slid in and braced. I rolled around and went in. The cabin was dark. Braced and ready, we waited. The only sound was the whisper of the wind in the trees outside.

Sid glanced at me, then shut the door. I holstered my gun and got out the flashlights. In the tiny circles of light they produced, we could see that someone had gotten in first and started trashing the place. Several cushions from a Herculon couch were scattered over the floor, and about two desk drawers had been emptied. But the rest of the room was intact.

I checked the kitchen. It was fine. A stairway led to a loft over the kitchen and living room. Sid was going through the desk. I went up the stairs.

A dark, wiry form leaped out at me. I dropped the flashlight and tried to dodge, but the stairs were too narrow. I stepped back, my foot hit air then slammed onto the next step. I was twisting to the side at the time, so I didn't go down. The form did.

Sid was waiting for him at the bottom, but the young man was quick and bounced up. He jumped at Sid, who dodged. The man clasped his hands and swung.

I was still trying to get my balance and over-corrected myself right into the banister. My side ached with the impact, but I didn't have time to worry about it because I was going over. I caught the railing just in time, then dropped safely to the ground.

Sid took a punch to the stomach, then landed two good ones in the young man's jaw. It didn't faze him. He came back, swinging wildly. Sid ducked, then worked in close and got the man in the stomach. I charged, and Sid and I caught the young man in a squeeze play. He struggled and almost broke loose.

We had a heck of a time wrestling him to the ground. I fumbled for the duct tape and tossed it to Sid, who had his knee in the young man's back. I got one arm. Sid got the other, and between the two of us, we forced them together. There was a ripping sound as Sid whipped the duct tape around the young man's wrists. I had to sit on his legs while Sid wrapped his ankles. I taped the mouth, while Sid found the flashlight I'd dropped.

He rolled the young man over and shone the flashlight in his eyes. Sid nodded at me and rolled the young man back onto his stomach. I took the flashlight, and as I did, I realized that the young man was wearing a blue and black flannel shirt, and near the bottom, a piece had been torn off.

Sid pulled me over to the desk.

"That's Donny Severn," Sid whispered.

"What's he doing here?"

We looked over the cushions and empty drawers.

"Looking for something," said Sid.

"Remember that scrap I found in my clearing?" I asked.

"Yeah."

"He's wearing the same fabric shirt and there's a piece missing."

"Hm." Sid glanced over at Donny. "We'd better hustle. Your dad and the DEA will be here any minute."

I hurried up the stairs. I found a couple hidey holes

in the wall next to the bed, and after a quick search brought the contents down to Sid. There were about three microdots and a three by five looseleaf notebook, and a heavy metal briefcase. I opened the briefcase and found a black box with dials on it and strapped to the case's lid, a disk.

"The transponder, I think," I whispered.

"I guess," Sid whispered back. "Let's take it anyway."

I showed him the notebook

"Records," he hissed, pulling a small camera from the pocket of his ski jacket. "You hide the box next to the cushions on the sofa, while I get this."

I set the box on the bottom of the sofa where the seat cushions should have been, then exchanged the microdots with three of the ones we'd gotten earlier. Sid snapped photos of the loose leaf notebook. I thought I heard a twig snap. I slipped to the front of the cabin and looked out a window. My father's large form slid onto the deck, next to another, equally tall, but slighter fellow.

I tagged Sid's arm as he took the last photo, and, grabbing the briefcase, we ran up the stairs. A second later, the front door opened and the lights went on. We dove for the floor.

"Hell," cursed the DEA guy.

"What happened?" grumbled Daddy.

"Somebody was looking for something."

With the lights on, Sid and I didn't dare look. We just hugged the floor as close to the edge of the loft as we could get.

The DEA guy cursed.

"That's Donny Severn," said Daddy. "What the hell's he doing here?"

"Leave him," ordered the DEA guy.

"What?"

"Obviously, another agency wants him. Look at this. Lehrer wouldn't leave a shipment out where anyone could find..."

"What you looking at there?"

"This box. It's the one Riordan was bringing up. She marked it. See, here's the serial number she put on it."

"I don't get it."

"She was supposed to drop it off at the store Thursday night or Friday morning after making contact with me, so I could tail whoever it went to. I had her mark the box to make it easier to trace."

Daddy cleared his throat. "Then how, pray tell, did it get here?"

"Della's room was searched. I checked that out Friday night. Damn it. There's counter-espionage people involved in this somehow."

"In drugs? How can you be so sure about that?"

"The tape. Lehrer didn't wrap Donny up like that. He'd use handcuffs. They're harder to get out of, and Lehrer has a legitimate reason for carrying them. Most undercover operatives can't get away with cuffs, but a roll of tape isn't going to raise too many questions."

"Huh." Daddy mulled that over. "So that's what Lehrer was talking about."

"When?"

"Last night, when he was putting in those bugs. He found a roll of strapping tape in my daughter's purse and asked if she knew what it was for."

"You mean Lisa?"

"Yes." Daddy's voice cooled considerably.

"That's... Yes." I could all but see the wheels turning in that guy's head. "It's about the only thing that really makes sense."

"What are you getting on about?"

"The tape in your daughter's purse." He laughed. "Bill, I think you've got a spy right under your nose."

"What? Lisa?" It was Daddy's turn to laugh. "You're talking nonsense. The girl couldn't even look at the body bag when they brought Murray out."

I felt Sid shaking with laughter, and jabbed him with my elbow.

"Trust me," Daddy continued. "She ain't got the nerve. The girl's a mouse. Her boss, maybe, but nah. She'd have noticed."

"He's got his hands up too many skirts, anyway. Playing James Bond is a good way to get killed."

I shook and got jabbed.

"So what now?" Daddy asked.

"We make tracks. They're obviously busting Lehrer tonight. Damn, I wanted his butt. Wait. I think we'll still get it. Here's what I want you to do. We'll go down to the Sheriff's station. You tell Lehrer you want to talk to him someplace quiet, and you want to do it tonight. Above all, you let him set up where it's going to be. I'll let you come with me to the meeting, but only to draw him out. I'll draw the attack. Come on."

A second later, they were gone. Sid and I got up. I headed down the stairs. Sid grabbed the briefcase and caught me at the bottom.

"Where are you going?" he hissed.

I wrenched my arm free. "After them."

Sid signaled me to wait, gave me the briefcase, then picked up the phone and dialed.

"Code nine," he hissed, and gave the address, and hung up. "Alright. We're done here."

He waited until I had dumped the transponder in the back of the jeep and got it going before saying anything.

"What the hell do you think you're doing?" he demanded.

"Saving my dad's butt."

"Get a grip on yourself, woman. We can't do a damned thing. If he sees either one of us, we're blown."

I thought. "Not necessarily. They're going to my spot. I'll just say you and I got in a fight and I was upset. I'll put the model thirteen in my jacket pocket. It should fit, and I'll be able to ditch it if I have to."

"Why don't we just let the DEA handle it?"

"Because it's my father!" I yelped.

"You don't even know if that's where they're

headed."

"It is." I glanced over at him. "That piece of shirt. Motley knew it. Murray was the one who showed me that place. I'll bet anything, he had Lehrer meeting him up there, and that's where Donny got roughed up, and alright, I'm guessing, but I'd say it's pretty safe that it was Lehrer roughing him up one way or other, possibly over Murray's death."

Sid sighed and leaned back in the seat. "Alright. It makes sense. And we haven't got anything else."

We parked off the road at the foot of the drop. The jeep blended in with the lighter colored rock, although it was screened from the road by pines. As we put on our other jackets, Sid kept watch.

It was cold. I shivered and folded my arms across myself. Down on the road, an engine thrummed and a set of high beams whitened the sky above the trees. Sid and I sat up, waiting. The car didn't stop.

Another car, coming from Nevada, went by. In the still following its wake, Sid gazed up at the sky.

"Look at all those stars," he whispered. "When I was a kid, I used to think that was where the other side was."

"What other side?"

"Death."

"You believe in life after death?"

He shrugged. "The first law of thermodynamics. Energy is neither created nor destroyed. There's been some interesting stuff coming out on out of body experiences. On the other hand, who knows for sure?"

Behind us, a small rock tumbled. We both swung around, Sid's hand reaching inside his jacket, mine for my jacket pocket. Another car hummed its way down the road from Nevada and kept on going.

Silence.

"He's not coming," said Sid, after we'd been sitting about ten minutes.

"Lehrer or Godot?" I asked.

Sid chuckled. Something rustled ahead. Sid

tensed.

"I thought the mountains were supposed to be quiet," he grumbled.

"That doesn't mean silent."

The bushes ahead rustled again. I caught a bouncing flash of white and sat back.

"What do you think that was?" Sid asked.

"A deer. Must be pretty confused to be this far down. It happens."

Sid pondered the skies again. I shivered.

"It's so clear," he said.

"No clouds. That's why it's so cold." I shivered again and pulled my jacket tighter around me.

Below us, a car slowed. Its lights went out as its tires crackled against the rocks and dirt next to the pavement. The sedan parked next to the trail leading to the clearing. Starlight glinted off the light bar on top.

"You win your bet," hissed Sid.

He was already out of the jeep. I jumped out after him and tagged his arm.

"This way." I nodded at the other side of the rock.

We heard the sedan's door open and close. Sid put his finger to his lips. I nodded. He took the lead, keeping me close enough to direct him and showing me how to get through the brush without making too much noise. I felt a little miffed. After all, I was on my home turf and he wasn't. [But you had never walked night patrols in a Vietnamese jungle, and I had - SEH] However, with Lehrer out there somewhere, there was no way I could argue.

The clearing was empty when we got to the edge. Sid's lips brushed against my ear. Thinking it was one stupid time to get romantic, I tried brushing him away.

"I'm going to the other side," he whispered so softly I could barely make out the words. "You watch from here."

Shaking, I put my hand on my model thirteen. Sid disappeared into the shadows. I waited for what seemed like an eternity. The clearing remained empty.

The brush to my right erupted in crackling and rustling, and I heard an "ooph." It was a fight, and someone had connected. Fearing the worst, I drew my gun and ran for the noise.

I saw the barrel flash almost before I heard the crack of the shot. Bark from the tree next to me exploded in a shower of slivers. I dove to the ground, aiming for the flash point, but before I could squeeze off my shot, the other gun flared three more times, with the shots getting closer and closer. I rolled, then lay still.

Wheezing, the stout heavy form crashed through the brush. I tried to get a fix on the shadow, but the next thing I knew, a rubber soled foot came down on my right hand. I swallowed the yell, then swallowed another as Lehrer fell on top of me.

I wriggled around, trying to get a grip on him. I caught polyester double knit and little else. I hung on and pulled myself along it. White light blinded me. Lehrer's hand clamped onto my sore right wrist. I gasped as he yanked me up.

"Well, what do you know?" he sneered. "I come up here trolling for Bill Wycherly, and what do I get in the net instead, but his kid."

I cried and struggled, but Lehrer's grip was like iron, and the flashlight felt like iron as it clipped my head. I sank to my knees. Laughing, Lehrer jammed the light under his arm and roughly cuffed my hands behind me.

"Don't hurt me," I sobbed, playing into my fear.

He backhanded me. "Shut up. You want to stay alive, you stay quiet."

He yanked me to my feet and all but dragged me to the clearing, keeping me at his side. He had a pump action shotgun under his arm with the flashlight. He dropped me on the boulder, then sat down next to me. The flashlight he propped up on his other side. Chuckling, he opened the gun and popped three shells in.

"Your dad should be here any time now. I was going to waste him from the brush, but now that I've got you, I might not have to."

The flashlight suddenly flew down the drop, and Lehrer was under Sid. [The dope had blinded himself with that flashlight right next to him - SEH] They rolled, then Lehrer landed on top of Sid, with his hands around Sid's neck. Sid popped Lehrer's triceps with his knuckles, then bucked and sent Lehrer flying over him.

In a second, Sid was on his feet. He dove at Lehrer, grabbing Lehrer's collar, then rabbit punching him. Lehrer went limp. Sid dropped him.

I staggered to my feet.

"You okay?" Sid whispered, pulling me off the boulder and leading me to the edge of the clearing.

"I think I've got a goose egg on my head," I whispered back. "Lehrer hit me with that flashlight. I feel kind of woozy."

Sid got one of the mini flashlights from my pants and waved the light in my eyes.

"Well, your eyes are dilating. You're probably fine." He put the flashlight back, then felt around behind me. "Oh, goody. Cuffs. Let's get sat down and I'll get you out of these."

He helped me to the ground, then popped open the sole of his left shoe and got out a tube of spring steel. A minute later, I felt the metal give around my left wrist. I started to wriggle my hand free, then Sid cursed and clamped it back.

"What?" I hissed.

"Your dad. I spring you now, and we're for sure pegged as operatives."

A light flashed on us.

"Lisle!" gasped Daddy's voice.

I couldn't quite make out the tall, slender form bending over Lehrer's body. All of a sudden, it dodged back and tripped as Lehrer roared to life.

Lehrer scrambled around, his hands landing on the shotgun. I got knocked flat under Sid as the gun blasted.

"Daddy!" I screamed.

The gun blasted two more times.

"Had enough?" snarled Lehrer. "Hackbirn, get off your girlfriend. Now! Move it!"

Sid slowly moved off of me. Lehrer came over, pointing the shotgun right at me. I howled as he grabbed my hair and pulled me up. He jammed the shotgun muzzle, still hot, under my chin.

"That hurts," I whimpered.

"It's not going to hurt at all when I blow your head off," snarled Lehrer. "Okay, Wycherly, what do you got on me?"

"I don't," said Daddy, struggling to keep his voice calm. "I just wanted to talk to you. Find a way to make peace."

Lehrer swore. "Say goodbye to your girl."

"Holy Jesus, have mercy," I gasped.

The gun went click.

I looked up. I was still under the stars, not among them. But before I could breathe to confirm it, I found myself under Sid, falling on top of Lehrer. Somehow, I scrambled free. But Sid and Lehrer were rolling on top of the boulder.

Lehrer pulled free first and got a hold of the shotgun. He swung it like a club. Sid danced back, then realized if he danced back any further, he'd be dancing on thin air. Catching his balance, he swung sideways. The DEA guy, whom I still couldn't see clearly, caught Sid, while Daddy jumped Lehrer. The shotgun clattered on the rock.

After that, all I could see was this pile of bodies heaving. It stopped slowly. The DEA guy got up first, then Sid, then Daddy. Lehrer struggled on the rock.

I sank to my knees, sobbing.

"Hey, it's alright. You're safe." Arms enfolded me, but they weren't Sid's. Or Daddy's. Nor was the voice.

The face slowly came clear in the starlight.

"Fletcher," I gasped. "What? How?"

"I'm from the Drug Enforcement Administration. I'm sorry, Lisa. I couldn't tell you."

"What the hell do you think you're doing?" snarled Daddy. His huge hand landed on Fletcher's shoulder and he ripped Fletcher away from me. "It's alright, Lisle baby. I got you."

"Oh, Daddy," I sobbed, laying my head on his shoulder.

"What's wrong with your hands?"

"He put handcuffs on me. Will somebody get these off of me?"

Only they couldn't. Fletcher searched Lehrer for the keys, but they'd been lost in the scuffle. They had to take me to the Sheriff's station that way, which was none too comfortable. Then it seemed like forever before they got a universal key up from the jail.

In the meantime, I had to go into another crying fit, explaining about the fight Sid and I had, which had made me so miserable I just had to find my special spot. Sid had followed because he was worried about me and to make up. They bought it.

My arms were really stiff when they finally got me loose. Sid started to move in to massage my shoulders, but Daddy cut him off. In fact, Daddy wasn't letting anyone near me, least of all, Fletcher.

There was quite a hullaballoo going on, too. Several FBI agents arrived with Donny Severn in custody. They were thrilled to find Lehrer already busted, but then a shouting match broke out between them and Fletcher and his cronies from the DEA over whose charges carried more weight. It was really kind of ridiculous because both the FBI and DEA are under the Department of Justice.

Once Donny saw that they had Lehrer, he kicked in, claiming that Lehrer set him up and Lehrer forced him to kill Della and Lehrer was behind Murray's death. When things finally quieted down, and someone had gotten the room service waiter from the hotel, Donny was put in a lineup and was positively identified as the gunman fleeing Della's room. He also confessed to killing Murray that Friday night because Murray didn't have his coke. He said it was an accident, that he'd hit Murray with the gun to get him to shut up.

I also noticed Sid and Fletcher commiserating and glaring at my father. When I finally got Daddy to find me something to drink, Fletcher came over.

"I want to explain about Thursday night," he said. "Della Riordan had contacted me about this back order she'd been asked to deliver to your father's store. It was actually a box of cocaine. I was trying to make contact with her in the bar when she stumbled onto your boss." He paused. "Yeah, I was trying to get into the suite, but more to get a hold of Della, than to make it with you."

"Then why did you stick your tongue down my throat?" I grumbled.

"I wanted to make it believable, and well, most women I know like it."

Sid smiled. "He's got a point, Lisa."

I glared at him. "You can stay out of this."

Fletcher shrugged. "Anyway, I kept trying to stay in contact because the coke had disappeared, and I was afraid Della had dropped it on you or your boss."

"Then who got it?" I asked. I'd already heard how it had been found at Lehrer's.

"We don't know," said Fletcher. "There were some undercover operatives working the case also. All we can figure is that they found the coke and dumped it at Lehrer's place. But with the code book that was found, it was more or less overkill."

Sid rolled his eyes. Of course, when we'd planted the box, we'd had no idea how important the code book was.

"Anyway," continued Fletcher. "I'd still like to stay in touch. I promise, no more tongues." He smiled sheepishly. "I really am a nice guy, and I have to admit, you were a nice girl to check out."

"Except she's got Atilla the Hun guard dogging her," said Sid. "And speaking of, here he comes."

Daddy wandered up and glared at Fletcher. "Here's a soda for you, Lisle."

"Excuse me, Bill," said Fletcher. "What are you so mad at me for? You've been raising hell with me since I said I'd met Lisa. I haven't done anything."

"You just stay away from my girl."

"Daddy," I groaned. "He doesn't have to stay away. It's my decision whether or not I want him around. And..." I looked over at Fletcher. Well, he was cute. Sid stood back, watching, with his arms folded and a bemused grin. "And I want him around. So there."

Daddy growled and shook his head, but let it be.

We left shortly after. Fletcher made sure I had his phone number and I gave him mine. Back at my parents' place, Mama, Mae, and Neil were still up and worried sick. So we had to tell them the whole tale. It was close to three thirty before my face hit my pillow, and by that point I was asleep.

September 24 - 25, 1983

My parents and Sid and I went to Murray's funeral the next morning. I got pretty soundly razzed when I wouldn't look at the body during the viewing. Daddy told us that Fletcher had thought I was an operative, and we all laughed. That night, Mary and Neff babysat the kids, while the six of us adults went to the casinos and gambled.

Sunday morning, I went to early mass, then Sid and I said our goodbyes and left. Mae and Neil were bringing Motley down for us because there wasn't room for the dog in the 450SL.

"Aren't we taking three-ninety-five back?" I asked as Sid turned the wrong way on the highway.

"Nope. We're going to spend a few days in San Francisco first."

"Oh. That's nice. But why?"

"Well, we have a transponder to drop off."

The metal briefcase was in Sid's trunk and had been since we got home Friday night. I didn't say anything because I could tell Sid wasn't finished yet.

Rain drops splattered onto the windshield. Sid drove through them silently, then turned on the windshield wipers.

"You know the line 'I'd give a thousand tomorrows for a single yesterday?'" he said finally.

"Yeah. 'Holding Bobby's body next to mine.'"

"Well, in a way, I got that yesterday a week ago last Thursday night. It was a beautiful night, Lisa. I have to admit, making love to someone as special as Della was, after all these years, and all I've lived through, it was very, very special. But..." He looked over at me, then at the road. "I guess, Lisa, I have a lot invested in you, too. When I consider the tomorrows we almost lost

Friday night when Lehrer pulled that trigger."

My heart skipped a beat at the memory. "I can't tell you how glad I was to hear that click."

"We don't have a thousand tomorrows, Lisa. We can't even count on a single one."

"Nobody can, Sid."

"But for us especially. Our lives are in constant peril from the work we do."

"Perhaps. I guess in a way, the future is the ultimate deception. It doesn't really exist, so how can we count on it?"

"That's exactly my point. All we have is the now, and to trade a future that is not even real to relive the past is the ultimate folly."

"Unless of course, you're putting the demons of the past to rest. But in a sense, that's not trading the future away. It's making the future possible."

Sid nodded. "And I think that's why we're going to San Francisco. We've got nothing to lose by it and everything to gain."

"'Nothing ain't nothing but it's free." I grinned and sang. "'Feeling good was easy, Lord, when Bobby sang the blues.'"

Sid reached over and squeezed my hand. "And feeling good is good enough for me."

I laughed and squeezed back.

Coming in Spring 2018

And now for something completely different. Here's a sample of my new mystery series, featuring Maddie Wilcox, winemaker and healing woman in Old Los Angeles –

Death of the Zanjero

We knew the value of water in Los Angeles. Back when our great city was still a tiny pueblo, water was scarce and our farms and ranchos were at the mercy of what the heavens produced. Back then we had to pay handsomely to have our fields and vineyards irrigated. Back then the Zanjero, or water overseer, was the most powerful man in the pueblo, which sadly meant he was often the most corrupt, as was Bertram Rivers. I had thought he was my friend.

The dawn was slowly lightening the surrounding hills as we gathered that Monday morning, March 28, in the Year of Our Lord, Eighteen Hundred and Seventy. It had been a fairly dry winter, but not disastrously so. We'd had a good rainy spell the week before, so the Porciuncula River was flowing and there was sufficient water in the Zanja Madre, the main ditch from the river that fed all the smaller zanjas that watered our ranchos and farms.

"Where in tarnation is that son of a b--?" Mr. Worthington snarled, then let loose a stream of tobacco juice.

The expectorant landed near my foot and from the look on my bosom friend Sarah Worthington's face, it appeared that her husband had aimed for me. I suppose a gentle reproof of his language and behavior would have been appropriate. However, it would not have been effective, so I simply stepped aside.

Sarah Worthington had come out with her husband to watch as Caleb Worthington and his men opened the sluice gate to my rancho. She was a tall, sturdy woman, with an elegant bearing and hair the color of freshly tilled earth. Mr. Worthington had been a miner before he and Sarah had come to Los Angeles and bought their lumber business. She was so dear to me, the first woman to befriend me when I'd been brought to this desolate place.

We were both anxious for the gate to be opened. I had been up all night and had yet to see my bed. Indeed, I was wearing my work dress, instead of a decent walking suit. Sarah had some matter troubling her deeply, probably Mr. Worthington. I suspected she wished to unburden herself to me, although I did hope that I could convince her to wait until later that day so I could spend at least a few hours in slumber first.

There were eight of us gathered at the edge of the Zanja Madre. Besides myself and Mr. and Mrs. Worthington, there were five workers. Two of them, Sebastiano and Enrique Ortiz, were from my rancho, the other three were part of the Zanjero's crew. The only person who was missing was the Zanjero, Mr. Rivers. He was needed to verify that the receipt I had gotten the previous Saturday did, indeed, reflect the amount of time I had paid for that Friday and to approve the opening of the gate.

As Deputy Zanjero, Mr. Worthington already knew that I had paid for my allotment, but Mr. Rivers refused to let anyone else open a sluice gate without his presence. Mr. Rivers said it was to protect the good citizens of the pueblo. I thought it a fine sentiment, but at that moment, one that was quite inconvenient.

"Perhaps, Mr. Worthington, you shouldn't wait," Sarah said, after hiding a small yawn behind her hand. "Else Mrs. Wilcox might not get her full allotment."

Mr. Worthington glared at her. He was as big

and burly as one might expect of a former miner, with dark blonde hair and small, dark eyes. He was wearing his usual dusty black suit and black tie. He spat out another disgusting stream, this time landing close to Sarah's foot.

"Hombres," he said, with an accent that was truly dismal. "Um, viy-eenay casa Rivers and officina. Diga Señor Rivers, uh, we're waiting."

As it happened, Baldo Vasquez, a short white-haired farmer, and Elias Padrino, a vineyard foreman with dark hair sprinkled with gray, both spoke English even better than Mr. Worthington. They glanced at each other, and at David Montero, a Negro who owned a good-sized tannery in town. Mr. Vasquez and Mr. Montero nodded and turned to do Mr. Worthington's bidding. However, they were saved by the appearance of Will Rivers, Mr. Rivers' youngest son.

He was a lad of thirteen, a tow-head with bright blue eyes. The boy usually wore what his three older brothers cast off, never mind that his father could afford to buy him new clothes. Will was very slight and his pants were generally tied on and his shirts constantly billowing about him as a sail on a merchant ship. One wondered how soon it would be before the wind would catch the garments and blow the lad away with them.

Will was barefoot, as he generally was, and approached at a dead run from the road leading into the city proper.

"Where's your pa?" Mr. Worthington demanded.

"Don't know," Will gasped. "He, eh, never came home last night."

That statement would have elicited a great deal more concern, but the pueblo was a rough place, filled with many temptations for those men who were weak-minded enough not to resist. That a husband and father should stay out the night was, sadly, not that unusual. I wouldn't have thought it of Mr. Rivers, but it didn't surprise me, either.

Mr. Worthington cursed loudly.

"Ma said to tell you to go ahead and open the gates today," Will said, trying to look braver than he was. "Pa will be madder than a wet hen if you miss your scheduled times."

Mr. Worthington glanced over at me, then at Will. Mr. Rivers did prefer that things be done properly. However, there were other rancheros waiting for their water and Mr. Worthington had other duties to tend to, as well. The tolling of the bell from the Clocktower Courthouse softly floated over the Zanja Madre from the center of town. It was six in the morning and time to give me my water.

"Hombres," Mr. Worthington finally yelled and gestured that they should open the gate.

It was a large panel of wood, painted over and pitched many times to keep the wood sound in the wet. Mr. Vasquez scrambled down the dry part of the brick zanja on my side of the gate and back up to the other side of the bank. Together, he and Mr. Montero and Mr. Padrino tried lifting the panel, but it was stuck solidly. Mr. Worthington took a long pole and began jabbing it around the bottom of the gate. The gate remained stuck. The three crewmen jiggled the panel and Mr. Worthington jabbed and suddenly the gate pulled free, upsetting the men. Water poured quickly into my zanja, rushing and whispering as it went past.

Then through the froth and foam, a dark shape rose up. It was the body of a man, clad in a dark suit of clothes. Sarah screamed but stayed standing. With Mr. Worthington pushing it with his stick, Mr. Moreno and Mr. Padrino reached out and as the water rose, were finally able to pull the body out of the zanja.

The man had been tall and broad-shouldered with dark blonde hair. There was a good solid cut and bruise on the back of his head, just above where his hairline had receded. His suit was torn in spots, presumably from the time in the water, as it otherwise looked to be of good quality. I looked over at Mr. Worthington, whose face had taken on a queer look. My stomach felt just as queer.

"Maddie, stay back," Sarah whispered, holding my arm. "It's too terrible."

I shook her off as Mr. Worthington turned the body over and confirmed that we had found Bertram Rivers.

Connect with Anne Louise Bannon

Please join my newsletter. It's the best way to stay up-to-date on my upcoming projects, blog posts and even games and giveaways.

Sign up on my website: http://annelouisebannon.com

Or connect with me on your favorite social media platforms:

Friend me on Facebook: http://facebook.com/RobinGoodfellowEnt
Follow me on Twitter: http://twitter.com/ALBannon
Favorite my Smashwords author page: https://www.smashwords.com/profile/view/MsBriscow
Subscribe to the Robin Goodfellow Newsletter: http://eepurl.com/zH0Ab
Connect on LinkedIn: http://www.linkedin.com/in/annelouisebannon
Follow me on Pinterest: http://pinterest.com/msbriscow
Follow me on Google+: http://google.com/+Annelouisebannonfiction

Other books by Anne Louise Bannon

I'm so glad you liked Deceptive Appearances! Check out my other novels, available in print or ebook at your favorite retailer:

Freddie and Kathy Series:
Fascinating Rhythm
Bring Into Bondage
The Last Witnesses

Operation Quickline Series:
That Old Cloak and Dagger Routine
Stopleak
Deceptive Appearances

Brenda Finnegan:
Tyger, Tyger

Romantic Fiction:
White House Rhapsody, Book One

And I would be honored if you left a review for this and any of my books on GoodReads or any other retail site. It really helps.

About Anne Louise Bannon

Anne Louise Bannon is an author and journalist who wrote her first novel at age 15. Her journalistic work has appeared in Ladies' Home Journal, the Los Angeles Times, Wines and Vines, and in newspapers across the country. She was a TV critic for over 10 years, founded the YourFamilyViewer blog, and created the OddBallGrape.com wine education blog with her husband, Michael Holland. She also writes the romantic fiction serial WhiteHouseRhapsody.com, Book One of which is out now. She is the co-author of Howdunit: Book of Poisons, with Serita Stevens, as well as the Freddie and Kathy mystery series, set in the 1920s, and the Operation Quickline series and Tyger, Tyger. She and her husband live in Southern California with an assortment of critters.

www.ingramcontent.com/pod-product-compliance
Lightning Source LLC
Chambersburg PA
CBHW070502120726
47910CB00003B/1098